A dark figure detached itself from the shadows

Bolan flung himself against the wall of the warehouse and drew down on the silhouette. He was a breath away from squeezing the trigger but checked his fire. The man just stood there, weaponless, legs spread apart.

Harsh laughter, then silence. Abrupt, cold silence.

"Mack Bolan, I have come for you. Do what you must. I will take you in the end."

Bolan heard in the voice the arrogance of a killer sure of his position, sensed the calm deadliness of a man who knew he could tackle any obstacle—and win.

Then the assassin moved with pantherlike speed and disappeared from sight.

A rustle of clothes preceded a squeak of rubber-soled shoes. Warning bells sounding in his head, Bolan looked over his shoulder.

Death came at the Executioner as twin flashes of steel arced toward his throat.

MACK BOLAN®

The Executioner

#60 Sold for Slaughter
#61 Tiger War
#62 Day of Mourning
#63 The New War Book
#64 Dead Man Running
#65 Cambodia Clash
#66 Orbiting Omega
#67 Beirut Payback
#68 Prairie Fire
#69 Skysweeper
#70 Ice Cold Kill
#71 Blood Dues
#72 Hellbinder
#73 Appointment in Kabul
#74 Savannah Swingsaw
#75 The Bone Yard
#76 Teheran Wipeout
#77 Hollywood Hell
#78 Death Games
#79 Council of Kings
#80 Running Hot
#81 Shock Waves
#82 Hammerhead Reef
#83 Missouri Deathwatch
#84 Fastburn
#85 Sunscream
#86 Hell's Gate
#87 Hellfire Crusade
#88 Baltimore Trackdown
#89 Defenders and Believers
#90 Blood Heat Zero
#91 The Trial
#92 Moscow Massacre
#93 The Fire Eaters
#94 Save the Children
#95 Blood and Thunder
#96 Death Has a Name
#97 Meltdown
#98 Black Dice
#99 Code of Dishonor
#100 Blood Testament
#101 Eternal Triangle
#102 Split Image
#103 Assault on Rome
#104 Devil's Horn
#105 Countdown to Chaos
#106 Run to Ground
#107 American Nightmare
#108 Time to Kill
#109 Hong Kong Hit List
#110 Trojan Horse

Stony Man Doctrine
Terminal Velocity
Resurrection Day
Dirty War
Flight 741
Dead Easy
Sudden Death
Rogue Force
Tropic Heat
Fire in the Sky

DON PENDLETON's EXECUTIONER

MACK BOLAN®

TORONTO • NEW YORK • LONDON • PARIS
AMSTERDAM • STOCKHOLM • HAMBURG
ATHENS • MILAN • TOKYO • SYDNEY

First edition February 1988

ISBN 0-373-61110-2

Special thanks and acknowledgment to
Dan Schmidt for his contribution to this work.

Printed in Canada

Alliances, to be sure, are good, but forces of one's own are still better.

—Frederick William of Brandenburg

The allies we gain by victory will turn against us upon the bare whisper of our defeat.

—Napoleon

In the killing grounds you need allies at your back.

—Mack Bolan

THE MACK BOLAN® LEGEND

Nothing less than a war could have fashioned the destiny of the man called Mack Bolan. Bolan earned the Executioner title in the jungle hell of Vietnam.

But this soldier also wore another name—Sergeant Mercy. He was so tagged because of the compassion he showed to wounded comrades-in-arms and Vietnamese civilians.

Mack Bolan's second tour of duty ended prematurely when he was given emergency leave to return home and bury his family, victims of the Mob. Then he declared a one-man war against the Mafia.

He confronted the Families head-on from coast to coast, and soon a hope of victory began to appear. But Bolan had broken society's every rule. That same society started gunning for this elusive warrior—to no avail.

So Bolan was offered amnesty to work within the system against terrorism. This time, as an employee of Uncle Sam, Bolan became Colonel John Phoenix. With a command center at Stony Man Farm in Virginia, he and his new allies—Able Team and Phoenix Force—waged relentless war on a new adversary: the KGB.

But when his one true love, April Rose, died at the hands of the Soviet terror machine, Bolan severed all ties with Establishment authority.

Now, after a lengthy lone-wolf struggle and much soul-searching, the Executioner has agreed to enter an "arm's-length" alliance with his government once more, reserving the right to pursue personal missions in his Everlasting War.

1

The safehouse was seconds away from becoming a hellhouse. Togged in combat blacksuit, the shadow that was Mack Bolan angled away from the wide dirt trail and melted into the gloom of the Colorado woodland. Unleathering the Beretta 93-R from his shoulder holster, the Executioner swiftly closed on the large wood-and-stone house. Less than a hundred feet ahead, three plumes of breath signaled to Bolan that his three-hour dogwatch had paid off.

Hitting a combat crouch in the brush on the outer ring of the safehouse, Bolan eyed the sentry. The M-16-toting hardguy stood guard beneath the balcony, twenty feet from the double doors that led to where the big session was taking place.

Bolan briefly recalled Hal Brognola's intel on this search-and-destroy mission. Five of the world's top dealers in black-market arms were gathered to plot the course of their next move, seek out their next clients. Brognola had not given Bolan much to go on, other than dossiers on the men involved and urgent words of encouragement. Bolan had mentally filed those names and faces away. He was there in the Rockies for a kidnapping. He wanted a pigeon, and he wanted that bird to sing. And Mack Bolan didn't much give a damn who it was who did the singing. There was a connection here to the world of international terrorism. Bolan intended to begin rattling the chains, then break the links later when the wild cards were in his cross hairs. Terrorist attacks in Europe and the Middle East, Brognola had informed him, had doubled, then tripled in the past six months. Someone was laying the groundwork for some horrific scheme, and Brognola's intel on the current upswing in international terrorism had turned Bolan onto the road that led deep into the cold wilderness of the Colorado Rockies.

Bolan watched the upstairs of the house for a long moment. Two shadows showed from behind closed curtains. Wary, even predatory eyes, the Executioner knew, were scanning the grounds. Several hours ago, he had counted the enemy numbers at the bottom of the trail. There were four more goons to deal with inside.

Bolan waited with agonizing patience until two of the three sentries on outside guard duty turned the corners of the house to make their rounds. Bolan drew target acquisition on the man left behind and caressed the Beretta's trigger. One silenced 9 mm parabellum chugged a true death line through the darkness. Muzzling at 375 meters per second, the slug cored through the man's chest.

The guy froze for a split second, then bared his teeth, as if he were trying to turn terror into rage and rage into action.

It was too little too late. Another whispering round for Bolan's Beretta blasted through the sentry's front teeth, punched out a hole at the base of his skull. A dark spray of blood washed over the stone behind the toppling sentry.

Bolan broke from cover and quickly crossed the thirty feet of no-man's-land. Six more hardmen remained, and Bolan wanted the heads of at least four of the five death merchants.

It was time to give the Devil his due.

In blood.

SENTRY NUMBER TWO FELL to the Executioner's garrote.

Coming out of the darkness, Bolan dropped the wire over the man's head. He crossed his hands, jerking the sentry sideways, making sure the M-16 dropped with a whisper into the brush edging the brick sidewalk. Reflexively the doomed sentry grabbed at the wire biting into his neck, slicing through jugular veins, vocal cords. Blood spurted away from the Executioner's death grasp, a crimson torrent that washed down the front of the sentry's shirt.

A door above Bolan slid open and rubber-soled feet padded down the rampart, alerting the warrior to another person's presence.

Bolan wrapped his arm around the torso of the dead sentry and hauled him into the deep shadows beneath the rampart. He waited, listening. Silence suddenly, except for the staccato chirp of countless insects from the woods beyond.

Finally the goon went inside. As the door above him slid shut, Bolan stepped out of the shadows, checked overhead and found the rampart black and empty. No sense in getting sucked in by the oldest trick in the book now.

The black-garbed specter moved swiftly to the back of the house. The numbers were tumbling fast, hard. And the nighthitter sensed a wall of doom and death that was set to come crashing down.

Beretta in hand, Bolan checked around the corner. Nothing. Darkness covered a patio ringed by a plant-and-vine-infested trellis. A boulder and a large air-conditioning unit and duct were just ahead. As he prepared to move across the patio to the double French doors, Bolan heard a twig snap. He froze.

The third sentry was making a thorough surveillance of the patio with a flashlight. As the beam roved his way, Bolan crouched behind the air-conditioning unit. The sentry inserted a key into one of the double doors. Bolan sighted down his Beretta and drew a careful aim. He knew he was taking a big risk by going for a head shot, but there was too much ground to cover to get to the sentry with the garrote. And if the guy got inside those doors, Bolan would be locked out. Time was critical. One of the boys upstairs was liable to discover the bodies. No, check that. Those bodies were *sure* to be found. The hardmen were pros, or they wouldn't be watchdogging the big five of the death-dealing trade. And if those guns played their cards right, they could hem Bolan in as he made his move.

The Beretta 93-R sneezed once, the slug cracking through the back of the watchman's skull like a hammerhead through an eggshell. The sentry's face slammed into the doorframe with a resounding thud. Bolan streaked across the patio as more deadweight crumpled at his feet.

He slid the doors open quietly and dragged the corpse inside, into the darkness. Locking the doors behind him, he headed for a hallway. Once there, light from the end of the corridor guided him toward the nest of vipers. Hitting a combat crouch, hugging the wall, Bolan padded down the narrow hallway. From around the corner he heard the voices.

"Then it is set, gentlemen. We have a deal. We had already agreed, then, on a date and place of delivery. Knowing how you gentlemen feel, everything was put into motion a week ago. I expect the shipment to be arriving anytime tomorrow after midnight. Their time, that is."

Bolan reached the end of the hallway. Judging the voices, he realized they were in the next room, the conference perhaps less than fifteen feet away from his position.

Bolan found that the hallway opened onto a dining area, and over the dining room was a circular opening in the floor that led to the second story. Wisps of cigarette smoke drifted over the railing above Bolan. Two wisps. Two of the four remaining goons. The groan of wood overhead gave away the positions of the other two hardmen.

"My men can have the, uh, industrial machinery moved from Apollo to Zeus as soon as the shipment is safely in port. I see no problem with the transfer then."

Bolan went back over Brognola's dossier. The first dealer talking must have been ex-Army colonel Thomas Darwin. A retired officer with an impeccable record, Bolan recalled. Impeccable, except that Darwin was a traitor who had sold his soul for reasons not even the big Fed back in Wonderland could gather. The voice of the second man had to belong to import-export mogul Gus Machelli. A mobster, Bolan knew, who was long overdue for the final cleansing.

"Monsieur Templeton, everything on your end must be secured, you understand, *oui*? My people are prepared to pay one half in cash upon arrival at Zeus for their portion. The rest upon safe transfer to Desert Base Allah. With this much ready cash on hand, there must be tight security. I will have my own people called in once Zeus is reached. I can afford to take no foolish risks at this stage."

Pierre Borbambeau, Bolan thought. International brigand responsible for the underworld sales of illegal arms to anybody and everybody, from the PLO to the IRA. According to Brognola's intelligence on the Frenchman, Bolan recalled, the man pledged no allegiance to anything or anybody. Except to the highest bidder.

Templeton was another ex-Army turncoat. A major who had gone the Nam route, then blazed through a long stint as a soldier for hire.

There should have been one more man there. Bolan had seen him earlier while watching the twin-turbine jets and Bell choppers land on the dirty runway in the valley. An East German. Friedrich von dem Bach-Zelewski. It was an alias, Bolan had been briefed, supposedly so named after the infamous SS general who had led the crushing of the Polish uprising in Warsaw in 1944. Exactly what Bach-Zelewski was, Brognola couldn't tell Bolan. The East German was a mystery. Supposedly an arms dealer. Supposedly a contract killer. Supposedly one of the masterminds behind an Eastern-bloc revolution and German reunification scheme. A lot of supposedlys. Bolan wanted to bag Bach-Zelewski and the Frenchman.

"There has been something set in motion that I must bring to the attention of you people. My own security in this affair must be assured."

Bach-Zelewski. Bolan listened carefully to the East German. Gauging Bach-Zelewski's voice, Bolan weighed the smoothly spoken words. But the East German's tone was clipped, as if he would begin barking out orders and demands at any second.

"As of a little more than a year ago, an urgent matter has arisen. The matter is Mack Bolan."

Hard silence. The East German had everybody's grim attention.

"Bolan. What about him?"

The East German chuckled. "What about him, you ask. Yes, what about him? His, shall we say, work is well-known within our circles."

"Just what the hell are you saying, Zelewski?"

"This. I am saying this, Templeton. All of us here stand to make anywhere from six to eight hundred million dollars on this deal. A billion, if all goes well. A lot of money. Money that will, that *must*, go toward the underground forces in East and West Europe."

"Christ. Here we go again. Get off the Fourth Reich crap, will ya, Zelewski? I'm getting sick of hearing how the Germans will be back with a frigging roar."

"It is not a bunch of crap, I assure you! Mock us now, but you will see, in time. The world will see. However, at this time I can ill afford any reversals, any setbacks. It has been told, time and again, and well documented within our circles, that this Bolan is a scourge. A scourge to be dealt with, particularly by men such as us. It is rumored that he is covertly working for Washington once again. Within every rumor there is some truth. Truth I will not overlook. And need I remind you, Colonel, Major, that your tracks have not always been sufficiently covered. There have been leaks in your pipeline. Leaks that were taken care of. But what is to say that this Bolan, the Executioner, has not gotten word of our operation."

"C'mon, goddamn it, spit it out. You're pissing away valuable time with all this—"

"Shut up! I cannot, I will not jeopardize my own pipeline as you Americans have. I have called in outside help. As of 0800 tomorrow, one of my contractees is on call. He will arrive and meet us at the sendoff. He will act as guard until, well, I have a gut feeling that Mack Bolan will make his presence known at some point. In that case, Bolan will meet his match in my contractee."

Bolan checked the railing overhead once more. He heard the creak of wood above as someone moved toward the railing. Plucking an MK-2 off his military webbing, Bolan decided to make his grandstand play. He pulled the pin and, with an underhand lob, pitched the grenade up and over the railing. As he armed the second MK-2, chucked the frag bomb over the railing and swept around the corner, Bolan heard a voice growl from above, "Hey, what the—"

The doomed sentry never finished the sentence.

Twin flashes of fire, and the blasts punched through half the railing, showering glass, wood fragments and plaster on Bolan. Screams ripped through the ringing concussive din, then bits and pieces of human flesh, chewed up by lethal razoring metal, flecked the wall, spattered the floor behind Bolan as he charged into the conference room. There, five very startled guys began to claw for leather.

Big Thunder roared onto the scene.

Like some avenging angel of death, Bolan filled the doorway. Two men in brown leather flight jackets peeled stainless-steel Detonics .45 Combat Master Mark VIs from shoulder rings. Bolan instantly recognized Darwin and Templeton from the pictures in their dossiers. Framed paintings of desert sunsets trembled with the thunderous retorts of death as 240-grain .44 slugs whipped through the air. The Army traitors became faceless, partially decapitated corpses. Skin and bone disintegrated, shards slicing through brains.

Short, stubby, dark-haired, mustachioed Gus Machelli turned a snub-nosed .38 on the invader.

Bolan showed him the final result that corruption wreaked on a man's soul. One headbusting .44 round was all that was needed to take Machelli out of the action. Permanently.

Suddenly Bolan saw a flash of something out of the corner of his eye. He saw the stiletto at the last second. The face behind that slim dagger was one of pure cold murderous intent. And those eyes, Bolan knew, had seen death delivered by the owner's hands. Many, many times. Bach-Zelewski.

With catlike speed, adrenaline sizzling through his veins, Bolan sidestepped the arcing blade. Zelewski missed, but the blade tore across Bolan's arm. Blood gushed from the jagged tear in his blacksuit. But Zelewski had just played his trump card. Bolan clubbed the East German over the head with the barrel of Big Thunder. Zelewski dropped, crashed through a flimsy antique lamp stand.

The last death dealer in that room leaped to his feet. Borbambeau thrust his hands into the air as Bolan swung the stainless-steel hand cannon his way.

"*S'il vous plaît! S'il vous plaît!* Don't shoot!"

"Give me one reason why I shouldn't."

Borbambeau's dark eyes were wary. "Because... because I am a rich man."

"I don't need money."

"Then... th-then name it. What is it you want?"

"Information. A lead-in to this big billion-dollar party."

"B-but, *monsieur*, how..."

Bolan decided to try another tack. "How would you like to take a walk?"

The Frenchman looked confused. "To where?"

"That's up to you, Borbambeau. We can either walk to the land of the living...or the land of the dead. The way I see it, you're already dying."

Bolan grabbed Borbambeau by the lapel of his silk three-piece suit, shoved him toward the doorway. A second later Bach-Zelewski began to stir. Bolan hauled the East German to his feet and jammed Big Thunder's muzzle under the man's nose.

"I'll make you the same deal I did him."

And Bolan did.

He had bagged his pigeons.

It was time for hard-core interrogation.

The man with the long white scar across his cheek checked his watch: 0805. He cursed. They were late, or had Assignment Damocles been called off? Damn, was he just killing time now, or was time killing him? he wondered. He hated to be kept waiting on anybody for anything. No one, he thought, kept a man of his skill and stature waiting. *They*—and it never mattered who *they* were—waited on him.

Clasping his long-fingered, big-boned hands behind his back, he took three somber strides away from his mahogany desk and stopped in the rays of sunlight that knifed through the skylight of his studio. Turning ever so slowly sideways, he gazed out through the long bay window. The oak sill was lined with edelweiss. More than two miles beyond the window loomed the snow-covered slopes of the Swiss Alps. Giant gray-white puffs of cloud ringed the jagged granite peaks. It was truly a magnificent sight, he thought, a crisp winter day when the sunshine seemed to freeze in the air. Surely a day when the Teutons, Goths or Vandals would have ridden out to conquer and lay waste to their enemies.

And Guntar Axeundarth was now waiting for the word to lay waste to a man he believed would be his most formidable enemy. A man who waged war safe and secure, Axeundarth thought, in the knowledge that his philosophy was the right one, the only one. The German believed he was destined to change that. Axeundarth would be his target's personal sword of Damocles. No, he had no reservations about taking this assignment. He longed for just such a challenge. Even though he would be paid one million dollars for this termination, the money was a secondary consideration.

Guntar Axeundarth knew he was the New Reich's premier assassin. How many men had he slain—a thousand? Two thousand? He had killed men with his bare hands, and with every weapon imaginable: from the Zulu assegai to the ninja *shuriken*; he'd ripped out a man's throat with a tiger claw and used a specially curved custom-made dagger for disemboweling. He was the best at what he did. But then again, the Germans *were* the best. Always had been, always would be. He thought anyone who was not of Germanic descent was merely subhuman. He enjoyed slaying Russians, Poles and Jews the most.

Suddenly the buffalo-horned telephone rang. He poured himself a shot of schnapps, then downed the drink. He fired up an Upmann cigar with a gold lighter. He took a deep drag, the harsh smoke filling his chest with a burning acid taste he relished for a long moment. Let them wait and wonder, he decided.

He let the phone ring twenty times before he answered it. Slowly he smoothed the black hair back away from his high, heavily lined forehead. Smoke wreathed his square-jawed, high-cheekboned face, and his gaze narrowed over blue-green eyes that glittered like diamonds.

"Ja," he breathed into the receiver. *"Ja... ja... ja... gut*. The hunting will be *gut*."

He placed the phone back on its silver cradle.

He stubbed out the cigar in an ashtray cut from South African diamonds.

He picked up a black felt-tip marker and scrawled on a large strip of white adhesive tape. He peeled the tape off the finely shellacked desktop.

Assignment Damocles was a go. It would be the crowning achievement for him. With that in mind, Axeundarth walked across the studio and opened a panel door set in the wall. He turned on the soft yellow overhead lights and walked down a wide corridor. Hanging from the oak walls of the corridor were swords, battle-axes, maces and knives. Authentic knives such as the Arab *jambiya*, the Gurkha kukri, the Finnish *puuko*. A replica of the sword of Isabella of Spain, a Persian sword of the 1500s, a Moorish boarding sword, the flaming sword of Don Juan of Austria, scimitars, rapiers, the broad-bladed sword of the ancient Goths.

Finally Axeundarth reached the end of the corridor. There, encased in glass, hanging from the ceiling by wire, were the trophies of some of his greatest victories. Stuffed. Embalmed. Memories of epic triumphs for his viewing alone, preserved for all time for whoever carried on his trade in his tradition.

The first head belonged to a KGB colonel, hunted down and garroted in Bulgaria. The collection included a Mossad agent disemboweled in Syria, an African dictator skewered in his own mansion with a cutlass, gagged, then stripped of his flesh. There were two dozen other heads, but at the moment Axeundarth was engrossed by the fantasy of what he knew would be his greatest victim.

The assassin walked over to a table and lifted an empty glass case. Guntar Axeundarth pasted the strip of tape to the base of the case.

He stood back for a moment, touched the scar on his cheek. Then smiled and looked at the case that would soon hold his crowning achievement.

Mack Bolan.

Yes, he thought. The hunting will be good.

"YOU CANNOT DO THIS."

"Just watch."

Mack Bolan believed that cruelty was for cowards who held the upper hand. Well, he held the upper hand, all right, but he had no real intention of going through with drawing and quartering Borbambeau. Unless, of course, the French arms dealer left him no choice. But Bolan had a gut feeling that the Frenchman would crack, long before the East German would spill his guts. In fact, Bolan suspected Bach-Zelewski would take whatever knowledge he had about the arms deal with him to the grave.

Jack Grimaldi, who had flown Bolan into the big valley of the Sawatch Range, stood beside the rented pickup truck. M-16 in hand, standing guard over

Bach-Zelewski, Bolan's old friend was once again the fly-boy for another hellfire mission. A hundred yards behind Grimaldi sat Condor, another warjet supplied by Stony Man Farm and handpicked by Brognola and Grimaldi. Armed with two 20 mm Gatling guns, one 40 mm and one 105 mm cannon, with four 7.62 mm miniguns fixed to the wings, Condor could become the ultimate bird of death in a split second.

Bolan fired up the pickup's engine. Black exhaust poured over Borbambeau and he cursed, straining against the ropes that bound his legs to the truck's bumper, his arms to the spruce tree.

Bolan released the emergency brake, revved up the engine. Angling his head through the driver's window, Bolan growled, "All I need to know, Borbambeau, is where those arms are going, who gets them, and what those arms are."

"Tell him nothing!" Bach-Zelewski spit.

Bolan looked with ice-eyes at the East German. "He'd better. If he goes to pieces over this, you're next."

"Go to hell!" the Frenchman yelled. "I'll say nothing. Do you hear me? Nothing!"

"Suit yourself."

Bolan dropped the truck into gear, slowly lifted his foot off the clutch pedal. The pickup rolled forward a foot, stretched the ropes and lifted Borbambeau off the ground.

The Frenchman screamed. The East German's lips curled back, and he appeared set to laugh at Borbambeau's suffering.

Bolan slipped the pickup into neutral and pulled back the emergency brake.

"Start talking, Borbambeau," Bolan warned. "Next time I keep going."

"*S'il vous plaît!* I talk. Fein Ali Husra! He is the Arab who will eventually get the shipment."

"You fool, tell him nothing! I'll kill you!"

Bolan stepped out of the truck. After several long, angry strides, he was looming over the outstretched Borbambeau.

"It is a new confederation of terrorists," the Frenchman blurted. "They call themselves the Spearhead of the Revolution."

"Silence!" Bach-Zelewski roared, then took a step toward Borbambeau. Then Grimaldi clubbed the East German over the head with the butt of his M-16, dropping the man to his knees.

"What are you shipping to these guys?" Bolan growled.

"Small and heavy arms. Rocket launchers, mortars, machine guns, even Stingers. However, a good part of the shipment tomorrow will be 7.62 mm ammunition and 105 mm shells for the howitzers."

"Miniguns? Howitzers?" Grimaldi breathed, a dark frown furrowing his brow and forehead.

Bolan didn't like the sound of this grim revelation. "For what?"

"C-130 gunships. Three Hercules are set to fly from Malta once the shipment of arms reaches its destination."

"Where is tomorrow's shipment going?"

"A port in southern France. Southwest of Bordeaux. From there, the shipment will be transferred to a château in the Pyrenees. There is a middleman, another armorer who has arranged the C-130 transfer for the Spearhead of the Revolution. A German. Heiselmann is the only name I know him by. But he has been my associate on a previous deal. I do not like the *Allemand*. He is not to be trusted."

Slumped on his knees, Bach-Zelewski looked at Borbambeau with pure hate in his eyes. "You will pay for this, Borbambeau, you spineless French swine. Breaking down like this now..."

"It is better to live to take your chances another day, my friend, than to die when you had been left with a choice."

"You just left yourself with no choice," Bach-Zelewski spit.

"Why gunships? What are these fanatics planning to do with them?" Bolan wanted to know.

"There is an underground movement in both East and West Europe," Borbambeau continued. "I understand it is a coalition between several of the major Arab and German terrorists. I understand they seek the overthrow of Europe and the Middle East, or they intend to annihilate everything. You see, a shipment of 105 mm warheads is due to arrive in Malta in three days. Nuclear warheads. For the howitzers. I do not know what they intend to do, I swear. But I have heard the alliance between the groups has threatened to break up because of inner rivalry. I know this, because I have been worried about getting paid for the delivery. Listen, I know nothing more of them, except that I am to arrange the delivery of the shipment to Heiselmann. I have my own principal purchasers waiting for their share of the arms shipment. I have my own people to answer to."

"Shut up! Shut up, or I'll kill you!" Bach-Zelewski screamed.

Bolan believed the French parasite, as far as knowing nothing more about the fanatic terrorist group. But the plan of attack now changed. Bolan decided he would have to get to Heiselmann, fast and furious. From there, the trail would have to lead him to the headshed of the Spearhead of the Revolution. Fanatics. Murderers. Conspirators. Whatever the German-Arab alliance was, Bolan intended to sever it, crush their evil ambition into the dirt. With nuclear payloads being delivered from the C-130s, Bolan knew the terrorist group could wreak death and destruction that most fanatics only dreamed about. And, if the right cities or military sites were selected... Bolan didn't even want to think about it.

Hell on earth, the Executioner knew, was just around the corner. It was time for the Bolan purge.

"We'll talk again on the flight," Bolan told his captives. "Let's load the plane, Jack."

"France, big guy?"

"Yeah. It's time to sink somebody's ship. Time to blow somebody's castle down."

"You do not understand," Borbambeau cried.

"Understand what?"

"If I am not at the dock tomorrow night, they will know something has gone wrong and will delay the shipment."

"It's a midnight arrival?"

"*Oui*. Or anytime after. Who knows? The captain is a notorious drunkard and malingerer. He is totally undependable. He's a wretch and a villain. . . ."

Bolan ignored Borbambeau's tirade. Sure, Machelli's skipper and plebes would be the scum who were steering the deathship across the Atlantic. They would be taken care of, soon enough.

"You'll be there, all right, bet on it," Bolan said. "And you'd better make sure all of us get greeted with open arms by that skipper. You copying on that, Borbambeau?"

"You listen to me! You will regret the day you ever met me."

Uh-huh, okay, Bolan thought, then reached for his commando knife. With the knife, he sliced through the ropes that held Borbambeau's legs to the bumper. The Frenchman hammered to the ground on his back, the wind belching from his lips.

3

Ten thousand feet over and two thousand miles across the Atlantic, Bolan was racking his brain for a plan of attack.

"Somehow... we've got to take them from the inside. Get in with one of these armorers..."

Grimaldi looked at Bolan, puzzled. "I oughta be afraid to ask this next question," he said, "but I've known you too long, Striker. What do you have in mind?"

"Infiltration. A hit from inside the ranks. Hell, Jack," Bolan said, his mind cementing itself on the problem, the task at hand. "Over the past years, this has developed into one of the worst law enforcement nightmares."

"Arms dealing to the terrorists?"

"Yeah," he replied, knowing he was long overdue in declaring all-out war on the major armorers of the world. A war, he knew, that might not end with the destruction of the Spearhead of the Revolution and whoever was fronting their operation with enough firepower to level a major city. "And it's not just the Soviets anymore. People on both sides of the wall are looking to get rich off the blood they help to spill. In our own backyard we got guys willing to sell out their own country for a buck. I hate to even think how many vultures are on Uncle Sam's payroll—supposedly upstanding citizens who are practically financing the bloodsuckers out there. Military men with the connections and know-how can feed these warmongers forever...unless they're stopped cold. The biggest part of the problem isn't the black-market arms, but the legal arms dealing. According to Hal's intelligence, arms-producing countries export seven hundred billion dollars a year in weapons."

Grimaldi gave Bolan a warm smile. "Sure, to help balance the budget. With all that firepower being exported, with all the money involved... Shit, Striker, you can't stop people from wanting to kill one another. You know that better than anybody."

Yeah, Bolan thought, animal man. Since the dawn of time, men have lived in fear of one another, wanting what the other has, willing to take it if he can't have it—the good man afraid that what he has can be taken, unless he's prepared to kill, and kill again. And animal man was there, right in his face, waiting to devour him.

War and conquest, victor and vanquished, seemed to be the greater part of the evolution of the species. Mankind isn't that far removed from the Dark Ages. Under the guise of civilization, the pretense of manners and love-thy-neighbor, the barbarian longs to break loose, impose his will on the weaker of the species. And running amok were the savages. Always had been. Always would be. Nothing ever really changed—least of all man's savage nature. Hell, Bolan had seen it thousands of times, lived with it for too long. Too damn long. And, at the moment, he was feeling as if he had lived with it forever. Damn, he was tired, bone tired. It was unlike him, he knew, to let the weight of the past, the knowledge of what the future most certainly held, bury his soul with weariness. And, yeah, even disgust over the human condition. The only thing that took that weight off his shoulders was hope. Hope that good men would keep fighting the savages who sought to trample underfoot anything that stood in the way of their own ambitions and desires. In his world, though, Bolan saw little hope. Mostly there was only struggle, a commitment to the grimmest of efforts to wipe the scourge of animal man off the face of the earth.

Bolan shook off his troubled mood. "What were you saying, Jack?"

"I was saying, what with all the terrorism running wild in the world, it's not hard to understand how a few C-130s fitted with howitzers could fall into their hands. But how? How in the hell could Templeton and Darwin have pulled it off?"

"Easy enough. They get to some people at the right places. Offer somebody a nice cut. Probably after they show him a few pictures of the husband and father who was somewhere he shouldn't have been. The guy gives in to blackmail. Has whatever weapons, or in this case C-130 Hercs, delivered where they want, when they want. The parts are probably shipped to a U.S. overseas base, where they mysteriously disappear."

"But this whole thing has to run a lot deeper than we've seen, Striker. You need someone with A-1 flying skills to pilot one of those Hercs. There's somebody else running the show. I'm convinced we're flying into a mighty big shitstorm."

"Well, it's a known fact that Russia supplies their Arab allies, even the Arab terrorists with high-tech weaponry. But they have to train, even use that weaponry alongside their Arab cronies."

"So you're saying the Soviets are at the helm of this one?"

"I don't know who's running the show, Jack. That's what I have to find out, and I'm going to start right now."

Bolan left the cockpit to interrogate his prisoners. Borbambeau and Bach-Zelewski were tied with rope, hand and foot. They sat with their backs braced against the wall of the fuselage.

Bolan gave the fuselage a quick look, wondering how many enemy numbers waited at their destination. One large metal bin, fastened to the wall in the aft of the warbird, housed the arsenal Bolan and Grimaldi would need for this war. Assault rifles. Submachine guns. Rocket launchers. An M-60. Two hundred pounds of thermite-coated C-4, which were earmarked for the freighters pulling into the French port tonight. A boiler-room blowout.

Bolan stood over the two men. "I've got a plan, and you two are going to help. Or be ready to take a swan dive out of here. We're ten thousand feet up. From this height, you'll hit the Atlantic like it was a slab of concrete. You'll burst like a melon."

Terror flickered through Borbambeau's eyes, and Bolan knew that he had his undivided attention. The East German didn't seem to give a damn either way; he had resigned himself to being a prisoner—at least for the moment. If the winds of fate shifted on Bolan, he knew Bach-Zelewski would come at him with every bit of murderous rage he possessed. As for the Frenchman...well, Bolan could see the guy wasn't ready to cash in his chips. Borbambeau was still the one to work on.

"I'm going to lay it out for you two just once. Any crap and you go out the door. Now...Borbambeau, you're going to show us exactly where Heiselmann is holed up. I intend to do a thorough recon of the area first. Then we go in for a meet. Here's the story. I'm free-lance help. Call me what you want—contract killer, bodyguard, whatever. But I'm there with you, as a partner. We deal together with Heiselmann. Upon delivery of the weapons to this Spearhead of the Revolution," Bolan said as Borbambeau's expression tightened with disbelief, "I will commit myself to Heiselmann to deliver five million dollars' worth of Uzis, rocket launchers, assault rifles, among other items. I'm the new kid in town, and I'm looking to move up in the pecking order."

"You are crazy!" Borbambeau cried. "It will never work. Heiselmann will have you checked out. He will discover you are a fraud. If you are, as you say, my partner...he will want to know why he has not heard of you."

"Let him check me out. It's a chance I'm willing to take. Because you're going to make me look convincing. You're going to back me all the way, guy. You've known me for years. I've done a lot of topflight work for you, and you're very, very grateful. I'm a trusted friend, the best damn muscle you've ever had. With my, uh, savvy, you feel that maybe it's time for me to branch out a little, go into business for myself. In other words, there's a big supply out there, and I'm going to help you meet the demand. Over the years I've established my own contacts, set up my own pipeline to different terrorist factions. All of whom I'm anxious to please. Their cause is my cause. I'm pulling the strings on this one, and you'll dance . . . or get your brains blown out on the spot."

"It won't work, Bolan," Bach-Zelewski declared.

Bolan noted the steely conviction in the East German's voice. "It better work."

"You don't seem to understand. There's a contract out on your head."

"So I heard," Bolan said. "Tell me about that."

Bach-Zelewski shrugged. "Why not? I know you overheard our conversation back in the States. And . . . I do not see what you can possibly do against our organization. We are too many, and we are too powerful. You are one man, no matter how good you think you are, no matter what your reputation is. If you kill me, someone will take my place tomorrow. If you kill a hundred of us, a thousand others will be there to carry on what has already started."

"You can fill me in on that later. First, who's coming after me?"

"The man who will be hunting you down is perhaps the world's foremost assassin. Perhaps you would even call him great."

"I wouldn't. You might."

"You mock me now. But your life is at this very moment dangling by a hair. You have been targeted as Assignment Damocles. Just as Dionysius of Syracuse dangled the sword by the hair over Damocles, so your very life now hangs in the balance. If you are *his* target, then I assure you, you will not live.

"I can give you no name, because no one knows who he really is. I cannot describe him, because no one who has seen him has lived to tell what he looks like. It is said he kills as swiftly, as silently, as the wind. When I want him I must go through the top-ranking officers of the organization. They, in turn, reach him by phone. On several occasions I have delivered his payoff. But my only contact with him has been in the shadows of a dark alley in one of Europe's cities—to hand him his money, and perhaps discuss the terms of his next assignment.

"I do not know how he will operate against you; he has no one pattern, which is one of the reasons why he is impossible to beat. No one knows him, how he will come or how he will kill. It is possible he will be at Heiselmann's waiting for you. It is possible he will be at that dock tonight, where you feel you will so brazenly walk up to the skipper of that convoy and announce that you are part of this...deal. *Ja*, go ahead, deal, Bolan, deal. You will die, that much I know. And I will be there, Bolan. I will be there to kick the dirt over your face, to mash your open mouth with the heel of my boot."

"That's nice," Bolan remarked dryly. "But the deal still stands, Zelewski. I start with your boy Heiselmann. From there, I intend to find out just what your *organization* is, and where it is."

The East German laughed. "You are a fool, Bolan. I give you credit for guts, but not for brains."

Bolan was finished with them for the moment. "Get your story straight, Borbambeau. You'll only get one chance. If you talk, people will start dying. And the dead will line up behind you."

With the baleful glares of Borbambeau and Bach-Zelewski on his back, Bolan stepped into the cockpit and sat down beside Grimaldi.

The ace pilot shook his head. "I've got to tell you, big guy...if you pull this one off..." He whistled. "What if this Heiselmann doesn't bite, then what?"

"What if he does, Jack? That's the way I have to look at it. We can't do this with a frontal assault. There are too many players, and they're too spread out. If I can get them all together somehow..."

"Yeah, but how? That's what worries me. You're going to be stepping into a situation where you don't know who could turn the guns on you and when. One leak, and you're history. So you get chummy with Heiselmann. So he buys your story—if the Frenchman can act convincingly. And I stress the word *act*. Heiselmann's liable to see right through it. And this wild card, this hit man, adds a whole new wrinkle. It stands to reason he's got a file on you. Pics. History. MO."

Bolan understood Grimaldi's concern, but he had already run all the principles of his warfare through his head. Objective: annihilation of the Spearhead of the Revolution and all parties concerned. Economy of force: an inside-outside blitz, with Grimaldi on standby. Security: gathering all intelligence, sifting out fact. Flexibility: go with the flow of the plan, dictate the action, but improvise when and where necessary.

Flexibility, though, was going to be the key to unlocking the trap he would eventually spring. But what trap? And where? And how? They were heading for one shadowy abyss, Bolan knew, with one foot on a banana peel and the other foot in the grave. But no victory, no true and lasting success, was ever gained without risk, without crossing the bridge of chance knowing that all could be lost.

Grimaldi was still shaking his head. "Too many ifs and buts, Striker. But...what the hell. We're here, and we're going in. Let's take it all the way."

Bolan nodded, staring out the cockpit window. Like sparkling diamonds, sunlight danced off the endless green waters. Looking off into the horizon, which stretched away beyond the rim of the earth, Bolan became suddenly aware of his own mortality. How many more blitzes into the dens of the savages could he survive? Surely, someday, somehow, somewhere, a bullet with his name on it would core through his brain. But, until that day came, he owed it to all the good soldiers who had gone into the void while giving their lives over to the good fight to carry the fire and the sword to the cannibals.

To do anything less, he knew, would be a crime. A crime against those who lived large and stayed strong.

"Yeah, let's take it on in, Jack. We're going for the big numbers. All the way."

4

Paul Arcadi was the only American in the cottage, and he was beginning to feel like a leper. As Gus Machelli's security arm on the European end for the weapons shipment, he was supposed to make sure the transaction went off smoothly, from the French port to the final destination. That meant making sure Machelli got the rest of his money when guys made the mad scramble to take what they wanted. The Europeans in the room knew why he was there, too, and they didn't like it. Or maybe, Arcadi thought, they just didn't like Americans. Tough.

Arcadi felt the sweat trickle down his back, as cold as ice. He looked around the room at the grim faces, careful not to let his gaze linger too long on any one pair of eyes. The eyes told him that he was not one of them, and he was going to be made to feel as much an outsider as possible.

There were six Frenchmen in the room, and at least one German, a hard-looking individual with an ugly white scar that jagged down the side of his face. A man, Arcadi was certain, who had turned more than one unlucky person into dead meat. The Kraut was a hitter, Arcadi thought, had to be. But why was he there? Who was marked? One of the Frenchmen? Himself? He fired up a cigarette to try to take his mind off that very definite and terrifying possibility.

"Your hand is shaking. Are you frightened? Are you nervous, my American friend?"

Arcadi found himself staring into the German's blue-green eyes, eyes that glittered like sunshine dancing over the water-slick body of an anaconda. Nervous? Arcadi thought. You're damn right. He glanced at the Frenchmen, all of whom were playing poker to kill time, and who seemed not to care that anyone other than themselves was even there. Worse, Arcadi thought, there were HK-91 assault rifles within easy reach of the Frenchmen, and they looked eager to trigger off a few rounds. Arcadi suddenly realized he wasn't just nervous, he was scared, damn scared. Of what exactly, he wasn't sure. But it was unlike him to experience fear in the presence of any man. And he hated these goddamn Europeans now for making him feel that way. He also got the distinct impression that, because they were European and he was American, they believed they were superior. Particularly the German.

With effort, Arcadi kept the quaver out of his voice as he said, "Hangover. I always shake the day after."

Guntar Axeundarth smiled. Slowly he moved to the window and pulled back the curtain. "I hope that the men you brought with you are not given to such indulgences the night before important business."

Arcadi felt a stab of resentment, recalling how the man had ordered his men to stand guard around the cottage. He was suddenly hating the scar-faced Kraut more than the Frenchmen, the urge to kill the German threatening to overtake his senses. But Arcadi shrugged, showed the man an easy smile and pulled deeply on his cigarette, the smoke calming his nerves.

"Hey, it's your show, boss. I'm just the hired help."

"So it seems . . . so it is."

Arcadi tore his gaze away from Axeundarth. For a second, he thought he saw one of the Frenchmen look up from his cards and smile at him with contempt.

"When did you say Heiselmann was due in?" Arcadi asked, hoping that talk would unwind the spring of tension he felt in his guts.

"I didn't. He will be here when he gets here."

Arcadi nodded, shrugged, as if he understood his humble place among the gods, but thought that when this deal had gone down he'd give the superior son of a bitch everything that he deserved.

Axeundarth turned away from the window. As he strode through the kitchen, he said, "I am going to check on your men. And check them—" he stopped by the door, looked back at Arcadi, a wry grin dancing over his thin, bloodless lips "—for hangovers."

"Be my guest. There aren't any goldbricks on my team."

Axeundarth, dubious, appeared to think about that for a moment, then opened the door and stepped outside.

Arcadi let out a pent-up breath. He decided he'd give the German a few minutes with his men. Then he was going outside himself to have a little talk with the man about his attitude. A real hard talk. Maybe he'd just blow away the Kraut right there on the spot. Because Paul Arcadi wasn't getting paid nearly enough to have to put up with that kind of crap.

AXEUNDARTH WAS ITCHING for some action. Killing action. It had been more than three weeks since he'd last killed a man. Too long. He felt his blood boiling with the urge to plunge a blade into a man's chest, or cut a pulsing throat with a razor, or pump a bullet into a target's head and scramble some brains across a lily-white wall. No, not even the cold air that he sucked into his lungs nor the icy drizzle that kissed his face could cool the fire he felt in his belly. A fire, he knew, that would never die. Never.

He thought about the arrogant Arcelli or Artini or whatever his name was, and decided he must make an example of one of the American fool's men.

Axeundarth checked the patio, then looked both ways up and down behind the cottage, finding no sentry there. Someone was going to pay for this negligence of duty. With his life. Negligence and incompetence were inexcusable. It was just one of the reasons, he thought, why America was a bastard country, full of mongrel races who had no culture or sense of history and heritage. Americans were shit.

Probing the woods with a narrowed gaze, Axeundarth found the example he was looking for. One of the American sentries was leaning up against a tree, his arms folded over his chest, his head lolling off to the side. A goldbrick, indeed—and the water that would douse the German's fire. Temporarily, at least.

Axeundarth felt an irrepressible smile stretch his lips. He reached inside his black leather flight jacket and slid the Walther PPK pistol from its shoulder holster. He imagined what he would do to the American, the look of shock and horror on the man's face when he realized death had come for him.

The German screwed a silencer onto his custom-built weapon. His stare fixed on the back of the target's head, Axeundarth padded into the woods. I am the hunter, he thought, closing to within a foot of his intended victim, you are my prey. I am Death, and I have come to take you. I am darkness and destruction. I am fire, sword and thunder.

Axeundarth stood behind the sentry for a moment, listening to his snoring. Then he wheeled in front of the man with the speed of a flash of lightning and dug his free hand into his target's crotch. He grabbed the sentry's scrotum in a viselike grip and squeezed with all his strength. The man jolted awake, his mouth vented, his eyes bulging with pain and shock. Before the scream could rip past the doomed man's lips, Axeundarth speared the silenced muzzle of the Walther into the sentry's mouth and squeezed the trigger. The pistol coughed three times, the .32 ACP slugs boring through the roof of the man's mouth, coring through his brain, punching out the top and the back of his skull in a spray of red-and-gray gore.

The body jerked in its death throes, then toppled to the ground.

Axeundarth was satisfied. He had just made an example for the other Americans. A German was in charge, a man who was to be feared and obeyed. Or there would be more killing. Plenty of killing. Axeundarth imagined that was what Americans were made for, anyway—to be killed, to be trampled underfoot. They were children, useless, crying children, all of them.

He looked toward the cottage, searching the corners of the safehouse for any sign of the other sentries, but found no one. Then the back door opened, and he saw Arcadi step outside.

Axeundarth holstered the Walther, picked the corpse up. He slung the body over his shoulder and slid deeper into the gloomy recesses of the woods, making sure the trees covered his retreat from Arcadi's searching eyes.

A hundred feet from the kill sight, Axeundarth gently laid the body down on the ground and covered his victim with brush and leaves.

He watched Arcadi for several moments, sensing that the man hadn't just stepped outside for a breath of fresh air. I should kill him, too, he thought. But he decided it could wait. The desire to spill blood would overtake him. Soon enough.

The assassin sat down, braced his back against a tree and shut his eyes. He felt the depression coming on, but it was always like this after he'd taken a life. It was something he didn't, perhaps couldn't understand. He reasoned that the letdown came from the sheer lack of challenge of it all. It wasn't like the old days, the first few kills, when he'd experienced the fear, the uncertainty, wondering just how good he was, wondering if he was any good at all. Testing his strength, his cunning, his ability. He had learned too quickly. He had become so skilled at stalking and killing a man...because he enjoyed it, and needed it. More than anything else in life. More than money. More than sex. Now it was too easy to kill a man. Or was he just that good?

Axeundarth reached into his jacket pocket for a cigarette, but a rustling noise alerted him to a new danger. The Walther streaking out of his jacket, he peered around the tree, saw three, then four shadows creeping through the woods, angling toward the cottage. In the murky lights and mist he couldn't make out the faces of the invaders. But he read the stealth in their advance, and he saw clearly the assault rifles in their hands.

It was a hit. The who and why would have to come later.

The German crouched in the brush. He waited until the invaders were a good fifty feet past his position, then shadowed through the woods on a course parallel to the hitters. He looked at the cottage, checked the tree line that ringed the safehouse to the east and discovered another squad of hit men gliding through the woods toward the cottage from that direction. He cursed because he'd left his HK-91 in the cottage. A Walther was no match against all those assault rifles in the battle he knew was about to erupt. Not even for Guntar Axeundarth.

He decided to hang back, observe how the situation developed.

There would be time to kill and kill again. Later. He had not survived as long as he had in the murder trade by letting the enemy or the target dictate the terms of a deadly encounter.

He who dictated controlled. He who controlled won.

Guntar Axeundarth could never fall beneath his expectations of himself.

He was the best.

BOLAN SHOVED BORBAMBEAU to the ground, then crouched, laying the black satchel, which was stuffed with a mini-Uzi, frag grenades, an MM-1 Multiround Projectile Launcher and eight spare 32-round clips for Little Lightning, beside him. They were now at the edge of the tree line, along the northern perimeter of the cottage. After Condor's touchdown about fifteen klicks north, Bolan and Borbambeau had legged it to the cottage.

A gray misty curtain of light rain slanted down over the field, the raindrops spattering through the foliage above the Executioner and the French armorer. The cottage was maybe fifty yards across no-man's-land. Quickly Bolan surveyed the cottage and its perimeter through high-powered Traq 10x50 binoculars. There were five sentries watchdogging the safehouse. Assault rifles were either canted to their shoulders in a lax attitude, or rested against the cottage. Two Peugeots, a Saab and a Mercedes were parked out front. A paved road led away from the cottage, cut through the woods to the east.

Bolan lowered the binoculars and stared icily at Borbambeau. "Okay, guy, you got your story straight?"

The Frenchman grunted.

"I take it that's a yes?"

"Certainly," he said, a sly smile twisting his lips. "My assistant, Mr. Maxwell. Free-lancer extraordinaire."

Bolan didn't like the Frenchman's tone. "Listen, if you get cute, you get dead. If you think you're going to blow the whistle and give me grief...well, I can take out more than a few of your buddies before they get me. And I'll blast my way through you to get to them."

"Whatever you say, *monsieur*."

The whole ploy was a deadly gamble, Bolan realized. If Heiselmann saw through the ruse, he would be left with no choice *but* to blast his way out with Big Thunder and Little Lightning. In the event he was somehow captured—and Bolan had no intention of being taken alive—a long-range homing device was taped to his ankle, and a miniature two-way radio was attached to the underside of his webbing. Grimaldi, sitting tight with Condor and guarding Bach-Zelewski would come gunning for the enemy next if Bolan was taken—or taken out.

"Do you honestly believe you can pull this off, Bolan?"

"If I didn't, I wouldn't be here. Besides," he said, giving the Frenchman a graveyard smile, "I'm going to be getting a little help from my friends."

Bolan gave the safehouse one final surveillance. He was ready to move out. Then he spotted more than a dozen men crouched in the woods, about twenty yards east of the cottage. Gunmen. And judging by the way they were eyeballing the cottage and the laconic sentries, Bolan knew they were poised for a strike.

Bolan handed the binocs to Borbambeau. "Take a look. That way. Ten o'clock."

A dark frown etched the lines deep in the Frenchman's face as soon as he looked through the field glasses. "They look...they look as if they are going to attack."

"Who are they?" Bolan gruffed, knowing the numbers were tumbling for a hardball engagement.

"How should I know?"

"Who might want to take out your buddy Heiselmann?" Bolan rasped.

"I'm not sure."

"Well, there's only one way to find out." Bolan dug his hand into Borbambeau's shoulder and hauled him to his feet. Unzipping the satchel, Bolan fisted the mini-Uzi, rammed home a clip and cocked the bolt. "Let's move it out, through the woods. We'll circle around."

"We?"

"Yeah, we. You're going to be by my side the whole time, come hell or high water."

"But...but there is going to be shooting. I could get shot! I could get killed"

"Tell me about it," Bolan growled, pushing the Frenchman away from him. Borbambeau hesitated, looking back at the grim-faced warrior in fear. "Move it!"

The thunderous retort of an explosion rolled across the field. Bolan and Borbambeau froze, heads snapping sideways. A roiling wave of fire obliterated the cottage. A second blast mushroomed into the sky on the blazing tail of the first explosion. Glass and giant shards of wreckage spewed across the field, debris cutting two of the sentries down like bowling pins. The other three sentries, stunned for a long and critical second by the blasts, triggered their assault rifles.

"Let's go!" Bolan snarled, grabbing the Frenchman by the arm, bolting through the woods.

Closing on the battle zone, Bolan heard the screams of the sentries, then saw the second strike team swing around the flaming wreckage and join their fellow killers in the mop-up. Assault rifles chattered for several seconds. Bolan watched as the hit teams mowed the sentries down with extended autofire. It was overkill, and the hitters were obviously enjoying the slaughter.

A minute later Bolan was in position to strike, securing cover behind a stand of trees on the hit team's left flank. Through the crackling flames that lapped up the wreckage of the demolished cottage, Bolan managed to make out the voices of the killers. They spoke in Arabic.

Bolan slid the MM-1 from the satchel and quickly loaded the twelve chambers of the weapon with 38 mm HE rounds. One-way tickets to hell.

Borbambeau's eyes widened with fear. "What are you going to do?"

"C'est la guerre, Pierre."

Bolan waited, drew target acquisition as the Arabs gathered around the four cars. One big, neat cluster, Bolan saw, as the hit team bunched up in a group.

He triggered the squat projectile launcher and one by one, a half dozen HE missiles exploded from the MM-1 within seconds. Two hellbombs turned the

Peugeot and the Saab into warped junk that rode the tips of fire tongues. Utter destruction, a flashing swirl of scrap metal and human meat, cycloned in a straight fiery line from left to right as the blasts meshed together. Bolan triggered another two HE rounds. More explosions pealed, spewing out glass and twisted sheets of expensive foreign car hulls. Screams ripped through the scorched, smoking air, lethal shrapnel lancing through the attackers now savaged by a firestorm that seemed to pour over them from the sky.

A group of nine survivors, several wounded, soaked in blood, scrambled away from the inferno.

Dragging Borbambeau behind him, Bolan stepped out of the woods. The Executioner wanted to bag a prisoner, and he would take that prisoner any way he could—shot up, busted up, or burned to a crisp over half his body.

Little Lightning blazed a lethal line of tracking fire. A swarm of 9 mm parabellum slugs chewed through the survivors, ventilated corpses spinning, slamming to the ground. A 3-round burst erased the face of another Arab, driving him back into the wavering flames of car wreckage. Bolan took out the last man with a 3-round stammer, stitching the hitter's legs with sizzling lead. The Arab screamed and nose-dived to the ground, clutching at his mangled legs.

Borbambeau stood rooted to the spot beside Bolan until the Executioner snatched him by the shoulder.

Bolan stepped into the midst of the slaughter, the Arab's cries of torment, the hissing roar of fire ringing in his ears. Hauling the Frenchman beside him, mini-Uzi in hand, Bolan loomed over the wounded enemy.

"Take a look at him," Bolan ordered Borbambeau. "You know him?"

The Frenchman's lips quavered as he stared down at the twisted mask of agony. He shook his head. "I...I do not know. P-perhaps... he is one of Fein Husra's men."

"Yeah. Perhaps."

Bolan spotted the movement beyond the wall of fire instantly. He swung the mini-Uzi at the figure stumbling toward him.

"Wh-who... who the hell are you?" Paul Arcadi rasped, grimacing, his hand wrapped over a blood-drenched arm, his face cut and gashed. He raked a gaze over the carnage. "And who the hell were they?"

"I was hoping you could tell me," Bolan shot back.

The Frenchman suddenly seized the moment. "I am Monsieur Borbambeau. I have business with Monsieur Heiselmann. I do hope he is not among... the dead here."

"Fat fucking chance of that. The guy's late... as usual. Borbambeau? We've been expecting you."

"Where's Heiselmann?" Bolan growled, as the Arab's cries faded to a steady moan before he passed out from loss of blood.

"Just who the hell are you s'posed to be, Jack?"

Borbambeau cleared his throat. "This is my assistant, and longtime associate, Monsieur Peter Maxwell, Monsieur, ah..."

"Arcadi. Paul. Machelli sent me and..." Arcadi looked at the bodies of his men. "Christ, how am I going to explain—"

"Heiselmann," Bolan cut in impatiently. "Where can we find him?"

Then Bolan spotted the two Mercedes-Benzes rolling down the road. Borbambeau and Arcadi followed the Executioner's stare.

"Could be you're in luck now," Arcadi said.

As the two cars closed on the ring of fire around the three men, Borbambeau, his gaze fixed, said, "That is Monsieur Heiselmann now. Heh-heh."

Bolan felt the icy hand of tension lodge in his guts. He looked at Borbambeau, who smiled.

The firestorm swirled around the Executioner.

But the real storm had only begun to brew.

5

A delayed explosion belched behind the drifting sheets of black smoke, and debris plunked down around the Executioner from the geyser of fire thirty feet away. Beside him, Borbambeau flinched, then grimaced in pain as flying scrap stung his face and neck before he covered his head.

While the two Mercedes were still a good hundred feet away, Bolan reached into the satchel. Quickly he slapped a fresh 32-round clip into Little Lightning. Just in case. The whip was about to come down, he knew. The charade was set to enter its first, and maybe last, act.

Moments later, both Mercedes parked outside the ring of fire. Doors opened, and eight men donning either black leather flight jackets or black leather trench coats stepped out of the cars. Gunmetal flashed as hardmen surveyed the carnage, and they looked to Bolan as if they were hoping to find a target. Something, anything to shoot at.

"Monsieur Heiselmann," Borbambeau called out.

Bolan steeled himself for a sudden engagement. Heiselmann was six feet tall and, Bolan judged, about two hundred solid pounds, with a square jaw that looked chiseled out of granite and close-cropped blond hair that swept away from a prominent forehead. Then, as Heiselmann pulled away from his entourage, Bolan coldly scrutinized one of his principal targets. Heiselmann, Bolan instantly determined, meeting the German armorer's stare, had eyes that seemed to judge a man on the spot. A man who knew himself and knew, too, what he expected, demanded, of anyone who associated with him. With his big-boned, slightly hooked nose, Bolan decided the German looked like a vulture and thought that the armorer had the right look for his line of work. The flotsam of the death dealers.

Heiselmann strode right up to Borbambeau and Bolan. He continued raking the Executioner with long and hard appraisal, then rasped in a voice thick with his native tongue, "Who are you?"

Borbambeau cleared his throat.

Bolan felt his hand tighten around the mini-Uzi. The stench of burning fuel, roasting flesh and acrid smoke stung his senses.

"This is Monsieur Peter Maxwell. He is my assistant for this transaction."

"Muscle?"

"Mmm, *oui*, in a way."

"Well, what way is it?"

Borbambeau was trying to play the game, but the Executioner determined he'd better butt in right away, in case the Frenchman began to falter.

"Free-lance. Name it, I do it. Name it, I've done it."

Heiselmann grunted, looking Bolan up and down as if he were some greenhorn trying to prove his manhood in the very real world where violence and death ruled day and night.

Heiselmann ran an angry look over the devastation. "Teuffel!" he barked. "I want a body count. *Schnell!* Now!"

"I bagged a prisoner for you," Bolan informed Heiselmann, then pointed at the unconscious Arab. "Right there. Mr. Borbambeau figured you would want to have a few words with the creep."

"A prisoner? For me, huh?" Heiselmann mused, his tone slightly sarcastic. "Just how did you two happen to come out of this in one piece, anyway?"

Bolan thought fast. "A little planning. A little luck. We were in the States, ironing out the final details—"

"I would rather hear it from Herr Borbambeau."

Bolan felt his jaw tighten, his heart thumping in his ears.

Borbambeau cleared his throat loudly, clasped his hands behind his back and rocked back and forth on his feet. "*Monsieur*, this is a most unfortunate occurrence indeed. My condolences go out to you for the men you have lost here. Unfortunately for your men, we were late in getting here. As of yesterday afternoon I was in Colorado of the United States. My security force, which also acts as my eyes and ears, if you understand, alerted me that an attack was expected on this safehouse."

"And how did they come by this information?"

"*Monsieur*, it is still being looked into, I can assure you. I am told by my security force that they received an anonymous phone call. A tip."

Heiselmann said nothing, looking at Borbambeau and Maxwell from behind hooded eyelids. Then: "So why didn't you bother to inform me of this?"

Borbambeau shrugged. "You realize, *monsieur*, that in our business, personal or direct contact is not immediate. There simply was no time."

Bolan tried to gauge Heiselmann for a reaction, but the German was giving nothing away by his expression.

"So you are saying you arrived here while the attack was underway?"

"Precisely."

The hardman named Teuffel reported back to Heiselmann with a body count. They talked in hushed tones, clipped German, and Bolan couldn't make out what they were saying. The gamble was well underway. And Mack Bolan could hear the black dice tumbling somewhere in the back of his head. If Zelewski's hit man was anywhere nearby, then Bolan was counting on the body of one contract killer turning up among the dead.

Or, Bolan knew, he would be among the damned.

GUNTAR AXEUNDARTH WAS NEARBY, all right. At the moment, he was shaking the cobwebs out of his head, rubbing his eyes and trying to clear his vision. Blood streamed down his face from the deep gash across his forehead, spilled into his mouth and washed down his neck. He spit, cursed. He was lucky to even be alive.

He hated luck. Luck was for the reckless and for the amateur.

Moments before the attack, Axeundarth had seen the hit team pull back into the woods. One of the attackers had said something over a walkie-talkie. Then, the next thing he remembered, the explosion had split the air asunder with its mighty peal. A piece of debris had hammered off his head and face, knocking him out cold.

Picking up his Walther, Axeundarth moved through the woods. His gaze locked on the firestorm ahead, and he spotted the men in the distance. Quickly but thoroughly he scoured the area around him for any sign of the attackers and found nothing but shadows and stillness. Moments later he secured cover, fifty yards east of the hellzone. His vision blurred, then cleared; his ears still rang from the explosion. He gritted his teeth for an interminable second against the waves of pain that stabbed through his head. This was no time to fall prey to an inability to shrug off the pain of wounds. This was a time for strength, a time to make himself all fire and iron.

As he focused on the tableau of men talking among the ruins of the battlefield, Axeundarth recognized Heiselmann, Borbambeau and . . .

Bolan!

For a second he thought he'd been knocked completely senseless by the blast. But there was his principal target, the dreaded Executioner, less than two hundred feet away. It couldn't be, Axeundarth told himself. There was some mistake. Why would Bolan be standing there with an Uzi, conversing with the major arms dealers of Europe? The Executioner and the Frenchman looked as if they were explaining something to Heiselmann. What were they saying? Something was very wrong. Or had some web of treachery been spun around him by the very people who had hired his gun? It had happened before. He had not survived this long by blindly trusting his associates.

Axeundarth spit out a mouthful of blood. He sighted down the Walther. It would be so easy now. One squeeze of the trigger, one dead Executioner.

No, it would be too easy, too unprofessional, the German assassin decided, allowing the Walther to fall to his side. Bolan was up to some deception. Perhaps the Frenchman was Bolan's prisoner. Perhaps Bolan knew everything about the arms deal. Perhaps the Executioner was even aware that he was now marked for death by the world's foremost assassin. Perhaps, perhaps. There were too many maybes. There were too many questions that needed answering before he made a move.

This was going to be very interesting, Axeundarth thought. And he determined not to make his presence known. Indeed, Heiselmann's gunmen were in the process of taking a body count. Fire would have charred many of the corpses beyond recognition. Therefore, they would assume Axeundarth was among the dead.

Then he saw the American idiot, Arcadi. Arcadi would know that he had stepped outside the cottage minutes before the attack. If Arcadi told Heiselmann that, then the armorer would assume that he was in on the hit, had perhaps staged the assault himself. So what? When the time came, and the time would come later on, Axeundarth decided he would make his deadly presence known to all, but only when he held all the cards.

And the Executioner would fall by his hand. Hard.

The hunt had to go on.

Timing was everything in the killing trade.

And the time was not yet right.

BOLAN SENSED that Heiselmann wasn't buying his story. And the mini-Uzi grew heavier in Bolan's hand with each passing moment.

"You know I do not like surprises such as this," Heiselmann informed Borbambeau, jerking a nod at Bolan. "Arrangements are always made through careful planning. I do not like dealing with faces I have never seen."

"Monsieur Maxwell has been on business for me for the past month. He has made some interesting arrangements himself for a proposed deal. And he finished his business sooner than I expected. *S'il vous plaît*, I trust you will hear him out."

"Later. Teuffel," Heiselmann barked at his henchman, "wake that piece of garbage up. I do not care how you do it. Piss on his face if you have to. But I want some answers. You see, I have been expecting to be hit for some time now," he told Borbambeau and Bolan. "It would seem I have allied myself with barbarians and traitors in these Arabs. Once again, it seems, I went against my better judgment. I detest having to deal with this trash. The fucking mongrel

Semites,'' he hissed under his breath. ''Heads will roll for this.''

Bolan tensed as one of Heiselmann's cronies began to inspect the satchel.

Crouching, the guy hefted the MM-1, looking up at Bolan with suspicion. ''Nice. It would seem you come prepared . . . for a war, yes?''

Bolan looked at Heiselmann. The German armorer's growing doubt was cracking new lines in his weathered face.

''Or to stop one,'' the Executioner returned.

As the Arab prisoner stirred to consciousness, Teuffel alternately kicking and shaking the man, Heiselmann joined the interrogation.

The German finished examining the satchel, and Bolan locked stares with the hardman for another stretched second. He sensed Borbambeau's mounting tension, glimpsed the sweat beads that had broken out on the Frenchman's forehead. He wondered how long it would be before the French arms dealer cracked.

''He is one of Husra's swine, I am sure,'' Heiselmann spit. ''Am I correct?''

The Arab cursed Heiselmann with a host of oaths in his native tongue, tears spilling from his pain-torn eyes. Heiselmann attempted to question the Arab for a full minute, but the wounded hitter just cursed and growled at the German.

''Ach!'' Heiselmann said. ''We will get nothing out of him. Kill him.''

As the armorer turned toward Bolan and Borbambeau, a single pistol shot cracked.

"Some real effective interrogation," Bolan commented.

The German stiffened at the barb. "It would have been a waste of time, Herr..."

"Maxwell," Bolan finished.

"Indeed. Herr Maxwell. I already have a feel for who did this, and I intend to retaliate. Perhaps not today, nor tomorrow, nor even next week. We are in a business, gentlemen, where no one can be trusted. Where no one is what they seem. There are rivals everywhere, competing for whatever it is you have, if you have anything worthwhile to take at all.

"I will not explain my actions to you, nor will you question my motives again, Herr Maxwell. Understood?"

Bolan nodded. No point in pushing his luck. He needed to get closer, bide his time.

"*Gut*. I believe we have some urgent business to attend to. However...I was wondering how you arrived here."

"By private jet, Mr. Heiselmann."

"Of course. Where is it?"

"About ten miles north," Bolan answered, feeling an icy finger tap down his neck.

"If you will allow me to drive you to your...private jet, we can make arrangements there to meet the shipment tonight. Once the shipment is unloaded and on its way, we will arrange to meet back at the château. There we shall discuss this, ah, deal of yours, Herr Maxwell. Agreed?"

"Agreed."

Bolan reached for his satchel, intent on flicking on the radio transmitter. Grimaldi had to know they were coming in with the players, or the game was over.

But Teuffel snatched up the satchel, smiling at Bolan. "Allow me, Herr Maxwell."

"Of course."

Bolan and Borbambeau were ushered toward the two Mercedes.

Another delayed explosion from the car wreckage boiled into the sky behind Bolan, parting the whirlwind of fire for a second. The stench of death bit into his nose.

6

They rode the ten miles to the Lear jet in silence. Bolan and Borbambeau sat in the back seat of the Mercedes, flanked by two of Heiselmann's gunmen. Through the mist and the drizzling rain the warrior made out the black bulk of the warbird, a hundred yards in the distance. Condor sat near the tree line that ringed a wide open field. The cockpit faced the oncoming vehicles, and Bolan's only hope now was that Grimaldi spotted their approach.

As the Mercedes pulled up in front of the jet, Bolan looked at Borbambeau, who was rigid with tension. If all hell broke loose now, Bolan knew that both he and Grimaldi would go down in the enemy cross fire.

"Nice. Very interesting," Heiselmann mused, stepping out of the Mercedes and walking up to the jet. He patted its fuselage, his men fanning out, surrounding the plane for their own personal "inspection." Turning, the German armorer looked at Bolan, his hand on the warbird's insignia. "A vulture?"

"Condor," Bolan corrected, standing beside Heiselmann.

"Ah, of course. The very large western American vulture."

The fuselage door opened, and Jack Grimaldi poked his head outside, looked at the men checking the miniguns beneath the jet's wings. "Mr. Maxwell. Mr. Borbambeau," he said, nodding at Bolan and the Frenchman in turn.

"Your pilot?" Heiselmann asked.

"James," Bolan answered, following Heiselmann toward the fuselage doorway as Grimaldi lowered the ramp.

Heiselmann raised an eyebrow. "James?"

"That's it—James. It's not his real name. Security reasons, you understand."

"Of course. Herr James," Heiselmann said, standing at the bottom of the ramp, "this is a most interesting plane...a warjet, I would call it? *Ja*. I have never seen anything like this. Would you mind if I came inside and took a look?"

"Be my guest."

Heiselmann and several of his men climbed into the Lear, Bolan and Borbambeau following. The Executioner and his ace pilot exchanged glances. As the Germans turned their backs to Grimaldi and began looking around the cabin and cockpit, checking the Bofors, he winked at Bolan.

Then Heiselmann pointed to the large metal weapons bin. "What is in here?"

"High explosives," Grimaldi replied.

"Such as?"

"C-4. Some spare 20 mm shells."

"May I take a look?"

"Listen, Heiselmann," Bolan growled, gut instinct warning him that Grimaldi had hidden Bach-Zelewski in that bin, "let's cut the crap. What's with all these questions? If you're accusing me of something, hell, if you don't like the way I look or don't believe I am who I say I am, spit it out. But we've got business to attend to. The inspection tour is getting tiresome. Besides, the inside of that bin is lined with high explosives itself. There's a timing device attached to it. You just don't open it with a key. Combinations have to be tapped, wires have to be cut. The whole process would take close to an hour."

"Very elaborate, wouldn't you say?"

"Damn right. With this kind of firepower aboard, we can't afford to take any chances with some fly-by-night marauder. Are you getting the picture?"

Heiselmann stared at him, his eyes as hard as flint. He appeared set to give Herr Maxwell a tongue-lashing, but smiled instead.

"I read you, Herr Maxwell—as a hard man who speaks his mind and means what he says. Your precautions are well-founded. You are a true professional, I believe. I like what I see in you—so far. But don't push it, and don't push me. What you have told me about yourself may or may not be true, and I can take nothing at face value, or simply believe someone at his word. As I have tried to impress upon you before, I can trust no man outside my closest associates. I have neither seen you nor heard of you before. However... there are those in our profession who operate best from the shadows. I understand that. And, with proof, I can accept that. Come," he told his men.

Bolan looked at Grimaldi, sensed that the breath was trapped in his friend's throat.

Heiselmann stopped at the doorway. Looking back at Bolan and Borbambeau, he said, "I will expect you both in Deuer Rochaine no later than midnight. Good day."

Midnight, Bolan thought, watching Heiselmann and his henchmen filing out through the doorway. The killing hour.

No one in the cabin spoke until the two Mercedes-Benzes drove away from the jet.

Finally Grimaldi let out a pent-up breath and slumped back against the wall.

Bolan unlocked the metal bin. Inside, Bach-Zelewski was bound and gagged, a dark bruise on the underside of his jaw.

"Good thing I wasn't caught catnapping, Striker. What's the next move?"

Bolan hauled a pack of C-4 from the bin. "This," he said, and began telling Grimaldi the next phase of the operation.

"I DO NOT LIKE this new development," Heiselmann told Heinrich Teuffel, his strong-arm and second-in-command.

They were driving through the Basque country, the Mercedes following a road that wound through the rolling green hills. France was truly a beautiful country, Heiselmann thought, suddenly wishing the Germans had kept it under their iron rule. Ah, the quaint Cognac farmhouses, the dunes in the northern Basque country laced with ponds and forests that seemed to stretch straight to the horizon. It was haunting, breathtaking country, Heiselmann decided. But he knew he could not allow himself to be captivated by the magnificence of nature's birth. Not when death was threatening to surround and crush him. But just what was it he was afraid of? He sensed trouble, deadly, ugly trouble ahead. A storm was building, and experience was warning him that he was walking straight into the eye of that storm.

Seated beside Heiselmann in the back seat, Teuffel asked, "How is that?"

"This...this Peter Maxwell character. I am not sure what to make of him. We should have been told.... We have done business now with Borbambeau for only two years. Still...we know his every move...."

"Or thought we did."

"Yes, or thought we did." Heiselmann's brow furrowed. "The body of Bach-Zelewski's contractee was not found in that mess back there?"

"It would be impossible to tell if Axeundarth was among the dead at this point. Most of the bodies were burned beyond recognition. We could have the bodies removed, checked."

Heiselmann waved his hand. "No. That would draw attention from the local police. We leave it. I will question this Paul Arcadi later. Let me ask you—was it me, or did I sense some tension between this Maxwell and Borbambeau?"

Teuffel pursed his lips and stared out the window at a flock of sheep being tended to by their shepherd in a distant field.

"There is something...not quite right there. You were not imagining the tension. Perhaps they were merely nervous because of your questioning."

"Perhaps." But Heiselmann didn't believe there was any *perhaps* about it. That Lear jet he'd seen was built for a specific purpose. What that purpose was, he intended to find out. There was too much money at stake now to be infiltrated by an outside free-lance operative, to be hit and have every deal he had ever worked to get himself to this point blown to the winds by some assassin working for a rival. But rivals, he thought, can be removed. And maybe this Peter Maxwell would help him crush the competition. All competition.

"Tonight," he told Teuffel, "after the shipment is unloaded, I want you to assign two of your men to Peter Maxwell. I want him tested."

"And?"

"There is no *and* about it. There will be a winner, and there will be a loser. If this Maxwell is as good as he thinks he is..."

"Then you intend to put him to use?"

"Exactly."

"So you intend to hear this...deal of his out?"

"Yes, I do. I have an idea. Perhaps he would even like to come to work for us. On a temporary basis. That is, of course, provided he is the one left standing after tonight."

"Of course."

"I believe we can use him in the struggle that is ahead of us. And, in so using him, in time we will come to find out just who and what he is."

A grim smile flickered over Teuffel's lips. "You do not believe he is who he says he is?"

"No, not entirely."

"Then what? You mean to hire him away from the Frenchman?"

Heiselmann cocked a grin. "For the right price, I can have the Frenchman eliminated. Perhaps, once I have the shipment at the château...I will. I never trusted nor liked the French. They are fair-weather in everything they do. In love. And in war. I will know soon enough if Borbambeau is trying to double-cross me. So, let us make an effort to become better acquainted with our friend Maxwell."

Yes, and a dance of death for the Frenchman, Heiselmann thought. That was how the acquaintance would become a bond. A blood bond of loyalty from Maxwell to Heiselmann. Unto death. It was time to begin eliminating the competition.

All competition.

7

Heiselmann's soldiers pried the tops off two large wooden crates with crowbars. Bolan and Borbambeau stood beside the German armorer. The cargo hold of the flagship *Alexandria* was a hive of activity. Crewmen toting assault rifles and small arms worked the conveyor belt of the self-unloading bulk carrier. Through the hatchway, Bolan heard the whir and groan of cranes and forklifts hauling the crates down the dock. Murder was being imported to the European continent and all points south. Bolan had to get to the receiving end of this shipment somehow.

He watched Heiselmann as the man hefted a Stinger rocket launcher from the crate. The Stinger was high-tech firepower, U.S. Army grade. A shoulder-fired infrared homing missile system, the Stinger zeroed in on heat given off by either a jet or a propeller-driven fixed-wing aircraft. Stored in a sealed tube, the missile was a weapon that required no maintenance in the field. With its heavy and deadly accurate firepower, the Stinger was a weapon that could turn one well-trained man into a one-man death machine.

The tops of other crates were quickly wrenched open. Heiselmann continued his inspection, his smile widening with each crate he examined. If a shark could smile, Bolan thought, then it would look something like Heiselmann. The smile seemed to stretch like rubber, and with the carnivorous teeth bared he looked as if ready to bite into the nearest bleeding victim. The guy was a savage, and Bolan wanted to drop him in his deathsights in the worst way.

There were M-16s with attached M-203 grenade launchers, M-79 grenade launchers, Mark 19 MOD-3 and XM-174 automatic grenade launchers. And, looking over Heiselmann's shoulder, Bolan saw a crate of what he was sure were 90 mm recoilless antitank rifles. Other crates housed Squad Automatic Weapons, the M-249. If ever a small war could be started, then Heiselmann was about to deal out the right stuff. Into the wrong hands.

And the armorer saved the worst for last.

Smiling at Bolan, then Borbambeau, Heiselmann patted a 155 mm shell. Judging by the size of the crate and the number of shells lined up on top, Bolan guessed that more than a hundred shells were in that crate. Just that one crate alone. How many other crates of 155s were in that cargo hold?

"This, gentlemen, is the big profit," Heiselmann announced. "I will have a count taken later, but we ordered exactly one thousand shells. Half nuclear. Half nerve gas."

"For the howitzers aboard the C-130s," Bolan said, forcing a smile he could never feel as he fixed his stare on the shells. With that kind of firepower destined to be unleashed from above by the C-130s on major European cities, Bolan knew that the Spearhead of the

Revolution could give new meaning to "urban warfare." If those shells ever... Damn, Bolan thought, the smoldering ruins of Stalingrad, Warsaw, Belgrade, Rotterdam would look like virgin white snowfall by comparison. Nerve gas and nukes. There was the grim and very definite possibility that millions could die in such an attack. And an even darker twist now gripped the entire scenario—World War III.

"Precisely. Now," Heiselmann said abruptly, "I want these ships cleared and the trucks loaded and out of Deuer Rochaine no later—" he checked his watch "—than 0400. I am taking my men with me now and leaving for the château to arrange delivery."

"I suggest I stay here and supervise the unloading," Bolan said. When Heiselmann raised an eyebrow, he added, "You've already been hit once."

"Herr Maxwell, take a look around. Every man here is armed. There will be no attempt in Deuer Rochaine to seize this shipment, believe me."

"Just the same, Mr. Heiselmann, I would feel better if I stayed behind. Then I can ride in with the eighteen-wheelers Hey, look," Bolan said, not bothering to hide his anger at the doubt he read in Heiselmann's eyes, "that's what I'm getting paid to do.'

"Very well. And you, Herr Borbambeau? You will be coming with us?"

"He'll be staying here with me," Bolan put in. "Someone's trying to hit us. I'm being paid by Mr. Borbambeau to see that he isn't taken out."

Heiselmann smiled his rubbery shark's smile at the Frenchman. "It would seem you have chosen excellent help Well, then, we shall be meeting back at my château. Until then,'' he said, wheeling and beginning to climb the ladder for the hatchway.

''Okay,'' Bolan told Borbambeau, ''let's go check out the operation, Pierre.''

''What do you intend to do?''

The clank and grind of machinery became a din that smashed through Bolan's brain with the shocking force of an artillery barrage. He felt the adrenaline dam up, keying him for the hit he knew was only hours away—the first major strike of many against this hydra of international arms dealing.

''I intend to sink a few ships, Pierre. For starters.''

BOLAN CHECKED HIS CHRONOMETER: 0358. Leaving Borbambeau tied up in the rented Peugeot, Bolan stepped out onto the narrow strip of rock and sand. The Atlantic Ocean, dark and calm, sent its waters lapping at the shoreline. Sea gulls skimmed the smooth black waters around the dark shadow of the nighthitter, seemed to cry out in one long mournful wail.

Crouching, the salty spray of breakers kissing his face, Bolan looked across the inlet through his infrared Traq binoculars. Two hundred yards north, the three freighters were moored at the port of Deuer Rochaine. Dark blocks of low-lying stone-and-wood houses stretched away from the freighters and the barges crammed into the harbor. A cool breeze carried the smell of seaweed, spices and fish away from the seaport town to Bolan's surveillance position, and his nose tingled with the heady scent.

At exactly 0400 Bolan counted sixteen tractor-trailers rolling away from the bays of the dockside warehouse. Moments later he saw a large number of the crewmen strolling down the wharf in groups, heading, Bolan assumed, for a café or the nearest brothel. Early reconnaissance of Deuer Rochaine had shown Bolan that the seaport was a wide-open, bawdy mini-Paris by the Atlantic, with women freely displaying their wares. The cafés had still been buzzing with coarse talk and drunken laughter even as he had set out for his current recon position an hour ago.

Bolan was about to bring lightning and hellthunder to Deuer Rochaine—C-4 thunder and thermite fire.

Those ships had to be sunk. Whatever weapon-wielding shadows he encountered on those ships would feel the Bolan fire. And the captain of the *Alexandria* was indeed going down with his ship. Even though the arms shipment was unloaded and already en route to its destination of death and destruction, the captain and crew of the freighter were responsible for this black delivery. And how many other deliveries? Bolan had to wonder. How many innocents had died because of what they had hauled for the late mobster Gus Machelli? They had to pay in blood. For this and their past crimes. And Bolan had to be certain those ships would never sail again.

Because he needed to deepen his involvement with Heiselmann, Bolan could not afford to leave behind witnesses to his strike. He would have to get aboard each of the three ships, plant the C-4 in the boiler rooms and leave like a ghost. If the German armorer got wind of the sinking of these freighters—and Bolan was certain he would—then Peter Maxwell would be just as shocked and angry as anybody else. No, Bolan couldn't afford to blow the charade now. He felt he was getting closer to knowing who would be receiving the imported firepower and where. But it might be to his advantage after all to tell Heiselmann the truth. And the truth was that he was evening up an old score with Machelli.

Moving back to the Peugeot, Bolan loaded up for the hit: Beretta 93-R with silencer, commando dagger, garrote. A mini-Uzi, also fitted with a silencer, hung from a strap around his neck. And, in case all hell broke loose, Big Thunder would ride quick-draw leather on the Executioner's right thigh.

Bolan hauled Borbambeau from the car.

"Wh-what are you doing?" he sputtered.

Bolan opened the trunk, forced a gag into the Frenchman's mouth, then shoved him into the trunk. "Just listen for the thunder," he said, graveyard eyes pinning the man to the floorboard for a second before he closed the trunk.

Several minutes later, Bolan was driving around the outskirts of Deuer Rochaine. Bolan parked a hundred yards north of the warehouses and slipped into a rucksack loaded with C-4 plastique.

He checked the area around the warehouse. Empty loading bays and trash bins. The bay area and its perimeter appeared deserted. Bolan set out, the silenced Beretta filling his fist.

Swiftly, silently, he shadowed down the length of the warehouses. Ahead, a lone lamp cast light down onto the wharf. Bolan kept his grim gaze fixed on the freighters, seeing neither sentries nor crewmen.

Then the dark figure wheeled around the corner.

Instantly Bolan flung himself against the wall of the warehouse, sighted down the Beretta and drew target acquisition on the silhouette beyond the lamplight. He was a breath away from squeezing the trigger, but checked his fire. The shadow man made no threatening move. Puzzled, Bolan waited. The man just stood there, weaponless, legs splayed. Bolan angled his body, searched behind him out of the corner of his eye, but found no one there

Laughter. Then silence. Abrupt, cold silence.

"You," the silhouette called out from the murk of night. "I am Death. And I have come for you, Mack Bolan. Do what you must. In the end...I will be there to take you. Take you into the void."

Bolan was sure it was Zelewski's hit man. The wild card in a deck stacked full of death. It could be nobody else. In the hit man's voice Bolan heard the arrogance of a killer sure of his position, sensed the calm deadliness of a man confident he could tackle any lethal obstacle and win. Overconfidence could be a lethal obstacle in itself.

Guntar Axeundarth chuckled, a dry, harsh chuckle that rumbled over Bolan's position. Then the assassin moved with pantherlike speed and disappeared from sight.

Why the games, guy? Bolan thought. Then he realized, as he had time and again, that a twisted killer's mind followed no rationale but his own.

Bolan padded to the corner of the building. Crouching, he checked the corner. The wharf was deserted. The assassin had vanished into thin air. Now Bolan knew he had to cover his own back during this encounter with the hit man. But Bolan intended to do some head-hunting of his own.

It was a good hundred feet across the wharf to the *Alexandria*. Sniper fire could pick him off before he hit the gangway of the mother ship. Speed. Silence. Daring. Bolan had to risk the run across the wharf. From his position, he could find no possible vantage point from which Zelewski's assassin could strike him down—unless the hitter had climbed to the roof of the warehouse. Bolan doubted that he had had the time. And there was no way he could have crossed the wharf already. All forklifts had been parked inside the warehouse as soon as the last eighteen-wheeler had been loaded, so there was nothing on the wharf a gunman could hide behind.

A rustle of clothes preceded a squeak of rubber-soled shoes.

Warning bells sounding in his head, Bolan checked his rear.

The two shadows surged out of the blackness.

Death came at the Executioner as twin flashes of steel arced for his throat.

8

Bolan threw himself back instinctively, but the two blades nicked the side of his neck, drawing thin lines of blood. The double-bladed attack, as one man followed his comrade for the swipe at Bolan's jugular, left both assailants exposed for a counterstrike.

But Bolan, burdened with the weight of the C-4, lost his balance, toppled on his back. He hit the ground, knowing he had only a millisecond to recover from his surprise and act.

The phantom attackers lunged at him for another one-two swoop at murder.

Bolan swung the Beretta around and squeezed the trigger. A 9 mm slug chugged from its silenced snout, coring through the chest of the man in his line of fire. He heard a dull thud and a sickening crack as the parabellum round punched through breastbone. One shadow went down. Forever.

Attacker number two advanced with the speed, strength and fury of a typhoon.

Bolan knew he'd never make it to his feet in time to escape the dagger plunging for his chest. Nor did his attacker give him the chance to roll away from the descending blade. As the enemy dived to pin his victim with his weight, the Executioner crossed his hands, thrust his arms up. Bolan blocked the knife hand, but the bone-jarring impact knocked the Beretta from his fist. Through the dim lamplight of the wharf Bolan stared up at a twisted expression of demonic rage and grim determination. With a heave of fury-powered might, adrenaline burning through his veins, Bolan shoved the attacker off to the side, and as he bolted to his feet, he saw the blade slash for his face. The warrior twisted his body away from the knife's edge, but steel sliced through the leather strap of the mini-Uzi, and Little Lightning clattered to the asphalt. Fevered by the instinct for survival, angry with himself for getting caught with his guard down, Bolan's hand streaked for the dropped weapon.

But the enemy kept surging with the speed and raw power of a cyclone. With one foot, the attacker lashed out at Little Lightning, kicking the gun halfway across the wharf. A reverse spinning kick followed, the edge of the attacker's boot glancing off the side of Bolan's head.

Face hammering into the warehouse wall, Bolan felt damp wood, stars dancing before his eyes. Then he felt the blood running, warm and sticky down his chest. Death had come to give, and Bolan was not about to receive.

In a berserk rage, the phantom attacker growled, rushed at Bolan, blade sweeping back and forth, charging as if certain he had a quick and easy kill.

Bolan pistoned a sidekick deep into the guy's gut, a horrible-sounding belch of air exploding from the attacker's gaping mouth. As the enemy doubled over, Bolan snaked the commando knife from its sheath.

The enemy's eyes widened in fear as Bolan's counterattack took a lightning and ferocious turn.

The wind driven from his lungs, Bolan's attacker was momentarily paralyzed.

Then the enemy's blade took a long but clumsy arc for Bolan's stomach. There was still plenty of speed and lethal power behind the intended deathstrike, and a lesser man with slower reflexes would have been disemboweled.

Bolan was no lesser man. With a brutal hooking motion, he showed his would-be killer Death incarnate.

The tip of Bolan's dagger tore across the man's throat, opening a blood-gushing yawn of flesh through windpipe and jugular veins. The body crumpled at Bolan's feet, twitched in its death throes.

Bolan rolled the corpse over, blood pooling around his feet. Instantly he recognized the face of the dead man and moved to check the other one. He had seen the second attacker before, too. Both had been Heiselmann's goons.

Questions burned through Bolan's mind. Did Heiselmann know the truth about Peter Maxwell? If so, where did that leave him? Bolan wondered, his jaw tightening from a sudden stab of apprehension. If Heiselmann knew, then would he go back to the Lear to kidnap or maybe kill Grimaldi? Damn! If the charade was over, then it was time to head out, guns blazing. Ask no questions. Take no prisoners. The numbers were tumbling fast.

Bolan returned his mind to the deathships in the present. Doing a quick recon of the wharf and finding it deserted, Bolan fisted the Beretta. Ignoring the fire racing over his shoulder from where the enemy blade had gouged flesh, the arm and chest of his blacksuit soaked with blood, Bolan ventured across the wharf, scooped up the mini-Uzi and hooked Little Lightning to his webbing. Sticking to the deep shadows of the wharf, he closed in on the first freighter. He crouched beside the gangway, checked the wharf, then the bridges and upper decks of all three carriers. Clear. So far.

Wheeling around the bulwark at the top of the gangway, Bolan found himself suddenly face-to-face with an M-16-toting sentry. The guy opened his mouth to sound the alarm, but the black-garbed invader gave the *Alexandria* its first casualty.

At point-blank range, Bolan drilled a 9 mm slug through the guy's head. Blood and brain matter exploded from the back of the sentry's head in a gory burst that sprayed the bulkhead. Bolan's arm streaked out like a black bolt of lightning, and he snatched the dead man before he could tumble in a loud thud to the deck. Quickly, quietly, Bolan stuffed the body into an empty drum nearby.

The main deck appeared to be deserted. Bolan knew that most of the crew was in town, sampling the delights of the flesh, indulging themselves. And why not? Their task was finished. Those who had not gone to town seeking pleasure would soon regret having stayed behind.

Bolan moved inboard, searching for a ladder that would take him belowdecks.

"Hey, who the hell are you?"

Bolan whirled, combat senses on full alert. Without hesitation, he drilled a 9 mm round through the man's forehead. The M-16 clattered to the deck, the corpse crucified to the bulkhead for a split second, as if it had been pinned there by the slug.

Hugging the bulkhead, Bolan reached the hatchway near the bridge, then lowered himself down the ladder. Once belowdecks, he checked the passageway, which was lit by four lamps secured to the bulkhead. The lights seemed to dance before Bolan's eyes in his adrenaline-pumped state of mind and body.

The black-garbed invader shadowed down the passageway, intending to search out and destroy the skipper of this deathship, intending to scrub free the one dirty hand that was washing the other.

GUNTAR AXEUNDARTH WAS on a search-and-destroy mission of his own.

The annihilation of Mack Bolan.

Moments earlier he had seen Bolan penetrate the security aboard the *Alexandria*. Penetrate by death. A fleeting shadow of fire and iron that was consuming everything in its dark path. Axeundarth found himself suddenly admiring Bolan.

Feeling strangely detached from the invasion of the mother ship by Bolan, Axeundarth leaned against the wall of the warehouse. It was interesting, he thought, to observe how the feared and famous Executioner operated. He put the flame to a cigarette. So far it looked as if Bolan would meet little or no resistance. The bulk of the crew of the three freighters was in town, sucking down booze and trying to get it on with the local French harlots. The German snorted derisively. Never mix business with pleasure, not even shortly after business was over. When a man thought that his job was finished, it was likely only beginning. Only iron discipline kept a man on his true path to destiny.

Axeundarth checked the time. He would give Bolan fifteen minutes to rig at least two of the boiler rooms with high explosives. After all, what else could have been in that rucksack?

Before Bolan hit the last freighter, Axeundarth would move out. He would kill anybody and anything he encountered aboard the third freighter. Yes, a warning trail of death for the Executioner. Stalk. Confront. Engage. Crush.

The German assassin screwed a silencer to his Walther. And puffed on his cigarette.

It was going to be a night to remember.

It was going to be a clash of titans. A lethal confrontation between the two masters of death.

Two men of fire and iron were going to engage shortly. Head-on.

BOLAN WALKED into the captain's quarters like a deck officer who had business to discuss. And Bolan's business was death. Discussion would be cold, brief and to the point.

At the sight of the black-clad intruder, the captain froze, the Scotch bottle poised above his glass. Bolan exploded the bottle out of the captain's hand with one silenced round, glass shattering off the bulkhead behind the man's desk. Shock and fear drained the color from the captain's grizzled, weather-lined face, a life-beaten, time-and-booze-ravaged visage that was made even uglier by the soft yellow glow cast over him by the desk lamp.

The jagged bottleneck trembled in his hand. "Who the hell are you?"

Bolan closed the door behind him and took a step toward the desk, a chilling smile curving his lips.

"A bill collector. Your tab's long overdue. How long?"

There was a ledger on the desk in front of the arms shipper, and a stainless-steel Colt .45 lay beside it. For a second, anger gave life to bloodshot eyes long since deadened by years of hard drinking. The captain's nostrils flared, as if he were a foul breath away from venting his outrage.

"How long *what*?"

"How long have you been shipping arms for Machelli?"

"What's it to you?"

"Your life. Or death."

Renewed fear tightened the man's expression. "What the hell do you want?"

"I thought I just asked you a question."

"Five years," the grizzled skipper responded gruffly.

"The right answer. But it's five years too long. Machelli's dead," Bolan told him.

"Dead? You?"

"Yeah. And I'm here to sink his ships. Make sure all parties concerned go out of business. How about it? You interested in going out of business, too?"

"Fuck you. You'll never get off this ship alive."

"I already got here. It stands to reason I can get out."

Bolan waited, saw the captain's eyes flicker over the Colt .45.

"You'll never make it."

"Asshole!" the captain hissed, his hand shaking over the desktop, scooping up the handgun.

Bolan's Beretta punched the unworthy sea dog a third eye. The man's head snapped back, smacking into the bulkhead.

"You were dead from the day you set sail, guy."

As Bolan approached the desk, the captain listed, then tumbled out of his chair.

The Executioner flicked off the light and left the cabin.

9

Bolan found the body at the top of the gangway. The sentry had been shot once through the forehead. Dead eyes stared up at him in accusation. Bolan wondered just what the hell was going on. Suddenly the night was alive with surprises. And danger.

Beretta in hand, Bolan looked inboard, then aft. There were no other sentries to be found on the bulk carrier. At the moment, anyway. But a crewman could stumble over the dozen corpses Bolan had left behind during his penetration of the other two freighters.

And C-4 was now planted in the boiler rooms. The attached time-delay activators were set to detonate the plastique in the *Alexandria* in exactly twenty minutes. Bolan had timed the explosives to go off on the ships at two-minute intervals. Result: confusion, utter destruction and the deaths of as many of the sea vultures who were asleep belowdecks as possible.

At the moment, though, Bolan was concerned with planting the last of the C-4 and abandoning the third vessel of death before doomsday lowered its hammer.

Moving inboard, Bolan found two more corpses. They, too, had been shot through the forehead, the dead left where they had fallen, right in the doorway of the galley. Okay, so the hit man was seeking out his target. That much was obvious. The gameplayer was leaving behind his calling card of death. The *why* of the ploy wasn't as obvious. Why all the cat and mouse? Was the hitter trying to put fear into his target's heart? Make him panic and sound the alarm on himself? If nothing else, then, Bolan assumed the stalk was intended as more a test of willpower and raw courage than the final confrontation, winner take all. Two could play the game.

Checking the corners of every doorway, turning and fanning the gloomy recesses of the passageway behind him with the Beretta after every four or five yards of advance, Bolan made his way past the bridge.

There was a stillness in the air that made him wary. He could sense the presence of death around him, nearby, reaching out its ice-cold skeletal fingers.

The living and the dead, the dying and the damned. Within moments, Bolan knew as he lowered himself down the ladder through the hatchway, it would be determined who was who and what was what.

And death once more greeted the black-garbed warrior at the bottom of the ladder. Three M-16-toting crewmen lay piled at Bolan's feet, their eyes wide and sightless, pale white orbs that seemed to burn as they mirrored the lamplight in the passageway.

Bolan, experiencing an unusual sense of morbid curiosity, decided to check the crew's sleeping quarters. There he found more pairs of sightless eyes staring at him. Berths had become coffins—men had been gunned down where they slept. The kills were so recent that blood still oozed from the wounds in chests and throats, spattered to the deck in trickling drops.

Bolan threw a quick look up and down the passageway, then stepped out of the sleeping quarters. Dead men were lying in each doorway. Was this supposed to be some show of cunning and strength? Was the hit man trying to prove he was just as skilled in handing out death? Bolan knew he was being watched. Perhaps even being followed at that moment.

The warrior found the boiler room and saw that it had become another proving ground. The engineers had been shot where they stood, either in the face or the back of the head. Pools of blood slicked the deck.

Bolan shucked off the rucksack, took out the last thirty pounds of plastique and set his mind to the grim business at hand.

BOLAN WAS halfway up the companionway when he heard the roll of thunder from above. His body tensing like a coiled spring, he trained the silenced Beretta on the hatchway.

Then the drum rolled through the opening, heading straight for Bolan.

The death hunt was underway.

Jumping away from the ladder, Bolan angled his fall out of the drum's plummeting path. The empty drum banged off the bulkhead, clipped a rung on the ladder and spun after Bolan. Hitting the deck of the companionway on his side, Bolan rolled, his teeth gritted against the waves of pain that tore through him from the bone-jarring impact.

A hollow boom echoed down the passageway as the drum crashed on the deck. After the echo faded, there was silence—a hard silence that hung in the bowels of the deathship.

Bolan swung his Beretta toward the hatchway. He expected the hit man to poke his face through the opening or come blasting into the hatchway, hoping to catch his quarry stunned and off balance.

But Bolan realized he could expect only unexpected, sudden and—if he wasn't prepared—lethal surprises from here on out.

Bolan moved down an adjacent passageway, heading portside belowdecks. At the end of the passageway he came to another ladder. He looked through the hatch and checked the deck of the forecastle. The night suddenly seemed to weigh down on him with the threat—and stink—of death. He checked his watch. *Alexandria* was set to erupt in less than ten minutes. Time to get the hell out of there.

But now he had a silent shadow dogging his every move, a killer prowling the ship with a hunger to take his life.

Bolan sprung through the hatchway onto the forecastle deck, the Beretta up and tracking. Cool air kissing his face, the smell of salt and spice stinging his senses, Bolan found that silence greeted him. The bridge was dark, an empty hull straight ahead.

As Bolan stepped away from the hatch, he saw the shadow wheel from around the bulkhead of the bridge. Years of living in the hellfields, where life and death were separated by a warrior's awareness and instant assessment of the enemy in a precombat situation, by cold judgment in the face of danger, saved Bolan's life.

He darted sideways, seeing the shadow draw target acquisition on him. Two silenced rounds whizzed past him, whined off the deck. Suddenly, as if outraged by his failure to kill with the opening round, Guntar Axeundarth surged forward and fired in a frenzy, the pistol chugging out another two rounds. The hit man had abandoned all strategy, opted for a lightning engagement and quick kill. Bolan didn't have time to chew over the assassin's change of plan.

No, caught out in the open, the warrior had no choice but to return fire with a fury.

Death was taking one of them.

Bolan's first 9 mm slug screamed off the bulkhead beside Axeundarth. The German assassin held his ground, triggered another 7.65 mm round that went wide of Bolan and tore into the rigging behind the Executioner.

Bolan squeezed off another round as Axeundarth retreated for cover behind the bulkhead and into the deeper shadows of the main deck. Through the murk, Bolan saw the hit man jerk, spin, then flip over the rail. A moment later he heard a splash as the hired killer plunged into the water.

Putting the hit man out of his mind, Bolan made his way down the starboard passage, then cleared the gangway in several long strides. At a dead run, Bolan made it back to his Peugeot in less than ninety seconds.

He checked his watch. Less than four minutes now to the first detonation.

Firing up the engine, Bolan drove down a road that ran parallel with the beach. A good three hundred yards farther from the wharf, he parked, hopping out of the car. Traq glasses in hand, he watched the *Alexandria*. Waiting.

It started with a low rumble, like the sound of thunder rolling in from the horizon. Then a geyser of flames jetted through the smokestack of the ship. On the heels of the shooting fire, thick black palls of smoke poured out of the smokestack. The *Alexandria* shuddered, then fire boiled through the hatchways on slick-looking thermite tongues.

Bolan lowered the binocs. Gaze narrowed, he watched the wharf and the town that ringed the harbor. Deuer Rochaine seemed paralyzed for a stretched second. Then dozens of men came running down the wharf, screaming, cursing.

Huge chunks of twisted bulkhead had exploded away from the ship, the jagged wreckage sinking beneath the surface of the black, silent waters of the Atlantic. Other sheets of warped metal banged off the pier, thudded off the wharf.

The second freighter shook with the tremendous force of the C-4 explosions.

Right on time.

More fire and smoke rocketed into the air. The black night sky was momentarily lit by brilliant flashes of orange-red volcanolike fire spouting from the smokestacks. Huge fireballs mushroomed away from the main decks.

Bolan waited, counting off the doomsday numbers in his head.

The last freighter blew its payload.

It would take some time before the deathships began to list. They were beyond saving, and there would be nothing left to salvage. Nothing but blackened hulls stuffed with the charred remains of corpses. The harbor of Deuer Rochaine would become their watery gravesite.

The savage who was in line for Machelli's job would get the message.

Loud and clear. In fire and thunder. And blood.

The cries of outrage carried across the peaceful Atlantic swells to Bolan as he climbed into the car and pulled away from the beach.

Bach-Zelewski's assassin was dead. Now he could move on to bigger game.

And the extinction of a deadly, thriving, savage species.

Animal man.

GUNTAR AXEUNDARTH WAS FAR from being dead. In fact, he had never felt more alive.

The German assassin trudged out of the surf, the waves slapping against his back. He stumbled onto the beach and dropped to his knees. His hand clasped over the hole in his upper chest, he gulped in the chill night air that the sea blew over him. Fire raced through every inch of his punished body. His head swam in a cloud of nausea. The bullet had bored through his body just below the left clavicle. Blood poured down his chest, and his back was soaked with the warm, sticky juices of his life's fluid, which gushed from the exit wound just above his shoulder blade.

Bolan was good. Very good. And Axeundarth wondered how he could have been spotted so quickly, so suddenly. It was as if Bolan could sense the presence of danger and spot it in the blink of an eye.

The three freighters were now swept by the raging firestorms, completely engulfed by an inferno that seemed to grow like a mountain that was being formed by some giant upheaval of nature.

Axeundarth could not suppress a smile. He admitted the awesome sight of destruction, and, grudgingly, he could not help but admire the source of that conflagration. Bolan was going to be a worthy kill.

Fire belched into the sky from the *Alexandria*. Already the mother ship was listing in the harbor.

It was good to see such destruction, and it was good to feel the agony he experienced from Bolan's bullet.

The pain would pass. Ships would sink.

And Mack Bolan would die.

Guntar Axeundarth climbed to his feet. He tasted the blood on his fingertips, licked his lips, savoring the bitter, salty taste.

A taste he found sweet.

Soon, very soon, he would taste the blood of the Executioner.

Next time, he would not be denied.

He had failed once, and he had never failed before to take a target down.

Failure. Another such failure, and he would be dead. All of a sudden, his own blood tasted very bitter and hateful in his mouth.

10

Fein Husra stared out at the vast emptiness of the Algerian Sahara. From a plateau high in the Ahaggar mountain range, he took a moment to pray for strength and guidance. This was a time of trouble. There was treachery among the ranks of the Arab-German alliance, and the reports from his sources in Europe indicated that he was soon to be embroiled in a major war with the German armorer. Husra felt he needed all the strength that God could grace him with for the dire time he knew lay ahead. There was going to be killing, plenty of killing. The road to paradise was about to become mired with blood. The blood of infidels. He would have his revenge against the German for the Islamic brothers who had been slain in France.

Beside the short, swarthy, bearded Palestinian leader of the Spearhead of the Revolution stood his brother, Fairak. A brother in blood, yes, but in more ways than that. They had killed together, many times, and each had saved the other's life more than once. In Damascus. Tel Aviv. Vienna. They had struck terror into the hearts of the infidels in those cities with car bombs, explosives sent through the mail, sniper attacks. Fairak was the only man on earth that he could trust with his life.

Moments ago, Fairak had broken the grim news to his older brother: their hit team in France had been annihilated. A report of the massacre had come from Fein's informants on the trail of the massive shipment of arms and explosives that was due to sail into the French port of Deuer Rochaine.

Now Fein was faced with a decision about how to proceed against Heiselmann. And what he decided could possibly seal the fate of the revolution.

"It is obvious that the German intends to set us up for a fall. This I have suspected for some time. I took the initiative, but he has succeeded in defeating me this time," he told his brother, tight-lipped, anger blazing in his dark eyes. "It is a shame—many good men were lost. But the bloodbath will be on Heiselmann's head next time. Brother, the hit was not a success because our men did not follow my orders. Obviously I must shake up the ranks somehow."

Fairak nodded solemnly. "I agree. What do you propose to do?"

A hot wind stirred across the plateau, swept burning grit over the faces of the men. Fein narrowed his gaze, tugged the green-and-gold *kaffiyeh* closer to his face. It was going to be another brutally hot day. A hot day in hell for someone—someone like Heiselmann.

The sun had already cleared the horizon and hung above the shifting sands, a flaming orange eye that seemed to suck the air from the desert straight up into the sky. The *sahra*. To the Bedouin the desert was home, a place of tranquility and beauty. To him, there was nothing beautiful or even peaceful about the desert. It was just there. A place where nomads had wandered for countless centuries. To Fein Husra, the desert was the boneyard of the Arab nomad.

"A suggestion?"

The brothers turned simultaneously, looked at the tall white-haired man in brown camous. It was Bernhard Dietl, a rival armorer, an undeclared enemy of Heiselmann.

Fein Husra liked doing business with the Germans because they delivered, and because they always did what they said they were going to do. It didn't matter if delivering meant shipping arms to him on short notice, not even in the bulk he had requested. It didn't matter if delivering meant killing infidels who needed killing. It didn't matter if delivering meant forming a solid plan of attack on a splinter terrorist faction and executing that plan so perfectly that every target was wiped off the face of the earth. No. The Germans delivered. They were conquerors, after all. Men of blood and iron. Warriors who, if they were to lose, went out with a roar and asked for no mercy. But Husra didn't trust the Germans. Yes, he liked, even admired what the Germans had done to the Jews during World War II. But he couldn't help but wonder what the Nazis would have done to the Arabs after the Jewish problem had been dealt with. The Jews and Arabs were, after all, descendants of Abraham. Children of the same bloodline.

But there was another reason why he couldn't afford to trust the Germans. He stared down into the gorge, and his dark mood seemed to gnaw through his bowels like the teeth of some voracious rat. Throughout the wide, far-reaching gorge, which was ringed by black walls of ancient rock, stretched his base of operation, his stronghold: wooden barracks; sandbagged antiaircraft batteries and machine gun nests; barbed wire; man-sized dummies for target practice; concrete tunnels and obstacle courses; prefab buildings used for mock assaults; fuel depots and water towers; three APCs; Soviet helicopter gunships and a transport plane lined up on the dirt runway, and an armory stuffed with weapons from both sides of the iron curtain, the instruments he needed to wage total and, he hoped, decisive war.

And he had the men who could use those instruments of death. With a feeling of mounting pride, he looked down into the gorge at the more than two hundred soldiers of the Spearhead of the Revolution.

Now those soldiers stirred to life. Shortly they would begin their morning drills. From the beginning Fein had been determined that the Spearhead of the Revolution would not be a hodgepodge operation, from training through to execution of the plan. His soldiers were here to learn tactics, hand-to-hand combat, knife-fighting, demolitions. They were to practice, practice, practice, and he intended to see them become the ultimate disciplined, efficient war machine. One that would thunder on to destiny like a runaway locomotive. A juggernaut that would crush anything in its path. Yes, he saw his Islamic brothers as soldiers who would fight for God as if they were automatons dealing death and destruction. If he had learned nothing else from dealing with the Germans, it was that discipline was the key to success. A goal, a plan, whatever. See it in your mind and stick to it to the bitter end. Never waver from your course, but drive yourself, and you will motivate those around you. Yes, Fein Husra liked the Germanic way of thinking. But then again, that was the larger part of his problem.

The entire operation here had been built and financed by Heiselmann, which meant that what the Germans gave, they could take back. But why, Fein Husra had to wonder, would they turn against him so suddenly, so violently? Indeed, the rumblings of treachery had come to him from clear across the Mediterranean. Some new Nazi Reich was in the embryo stage and growing stronger daily. That had to be the reason for the web of treachery that was being spun around him. So... he had been set up by Heiselmann. Used. And soon to be discarded. Was his base here in the Sahara merely a stepping-stone for the Germans, a hideout? Or perhaps it was intended to be used as their own base of operations from which they could launch assaults. If this was true, then that explained why he had been able to negotiate for the C-130s with so little trouble.

It also helped that he was now being funded by Libyan oil money and could afford to deal with the Germans from his own financial base. It had been very smart on his part to go to the Libyans months ago and form that bond. Money in exchange for exporting terrorism. That was the deal. And the colonel's cronies had been only too willing to cooperate. The Libyans were, after all, brothers in blood also, waging a bitter struggle against the infidels, the Western warmongers and their Israeli lapdogs.

"Tell me, Dietl, what is your suggestion?"

Dietl adjusted his dark aviator shades and cleared his throat. "A kidnapping."

"A kidnapping? Who?"

"Simple. Heiselmann. You know and I know that Heiselmann and myself are bitter enemies. He squeezed me out of a deal years ago that nearly bankrupted my operation. I have recouped my losses only because I have acquired an excellent team of...hitters over the years. Contract killers. Mercenaries. All of them organized, trained in paramilitary operations and led by three former GSG-9 men. Without them, I would not have been able to acquire new territory. In a way I owe them. And by letting them flex some muscle...well, let us say I would be paying back my debt by putting them to use, you see."

When Dietl paused, Fein said, "Continue. I'm listening."

Again Dietl cleared his throat, remaining silent for a long moment. It was obvious that the German did not like being talked to in such an authoritative tone. Tough, the Palestinian thought.

"I suggest you let me handle this delicate operation."

Fairak Husra snorted. "You're crazy. After what has gone down in France! Any action taken against Heiselmann will have to be approved by us," he snarled, his voice trembling with rage.

"Brother, brother, please," Fein said, holding up his hand in a gesture that asked for restraint. "I agree with my brother, Dietl. But I cannot trust any man who operates outside of our circle here. Not until the C-130s are delivered as promised by Heiselmann."

"Therein lies the problem."

"Explain."

"You must get the C-130s first. If Heiselmann knows you were responsible for the failed attack, then what makes you think he will deal straight with you from now on?" Dietl paused, turned and looked at the Husras.

The Palestinians were silent. The German had made a good point. And he was on to something of importance.

"I can have my men," Dietl continued, "kidnap Heiselmann from his château in the Pyrenees."

Fein Husra was astonished. "How?"

"Have you ever heard of Eben Amael?"

"Yes," Fein growled. "The Belgian fortress that was supposedly impenetrable. German paratroopers landed on the roof of the fortress in gliders and took it before the defenders knew what happened."

"*Ja*, exactly. And all of them Iron Cross winners," he added under his breath, gazing out at the desert, wondering if he was Iron Cross material himself. Then, abruptly, he cleared his throat, continued. "So, too, my men are highly trained in the use of gliders as assault vehicles. Reconnaissance has already been done on the château. In fact, I have been planning this operation for six months. I held off when I heard the rumor about the C-130s."

Fein looked at Dietl suspiciously. "Why?"

Dietl shrugged, chuckled. "My friend, you have nothing to fear from me. I merely want Heiselmann out of the picture. For good. Surely you of all people can understand the need for vengeance. With Heiselmann as your hostage you can make sure that those planes and the rest of the armament is delivered here. You will have the planes, Heiselmann . . . and, if you work it right and allow me some input, you can keep every last franc you would owe him."

"Let me think about it."

"Do not take too long, my friend. I leave within the hour."

Fein Husra drew a deep breath, the parched dry air stinging his nose and throat. The German had a good plan, and he liked it. Better still, he knew the Germans would make it work. He had known all along that Heiselmann was going to double-cross him on this C-130 deal. Yes, if Heiselmann would double-cross one of his own, then what would stop him from doing it to an Arab? The alliance had been shaky from the start, and Fein was looking for an excuse, any excuse to sever relations with the Germans. The Germans had their own interests—whatever they might be—and he was not privy to intelligence on whatever goals they had in mind. But he knew what the Spearhead of the Revolution must do—the group had its own destiny to fulfill. Why, with the C130s . . . No! There was something he had not thought of until now. Heiselmann had promised to deliver the pilots for those C-130s. They were being trained and housed in Crete, or Malta, he wasn't sure exactly where. What would he do now? Without Heiselmann's pilots the C-130s might never take off. And he was anxious to launch the attacks on the targeted European cities. It would take months, maybe even a year or more before he found the right pilots again. And he hated having to go to the Soviets. They were every bit as arrogant and hostile as the Germans. Worse, they always made him feel as if he should go to them on bended knee, groveling and begging for help in the sacred name of the almighty Kremlin. Yes, he thought, the Russians believed Arabs were nothing more than a tool to be used against the West. And when the Russians felt an Arab group had outlived its usefulness to the Kremlin, then it was nothing more than something to be wiped off the bottom of their boots.

"Pilots," Fein Husra hissed, unaware that he was speaking his thoughts.

"Pilots?"

"Yes, pilots. Heiselmann also promised to deliver the men who would fly the C-130s."

"Relax. All of that will be taken care of. The kidnapping, believe me, will bring you those pilots, also."

"Then you arrange this kidnapping, Dietl. When can it be done?"

"Immediately. I will order my team to hit the château as soon as I leave here."

"I want a team of my own men to go along," Fein demanded.

"You do not trust me?"

"Let's just say I will feel better knowing my own people are involved in this kidnapping."

A thin smile slashed Dietl's lips. "Very well. Sort of like . . . team spirit."

"Go, then," Fein said. "I have arrangements of my own to make."

Dietl nodded, his jaws clenching. He wheeled and strode away from the Husra brothers.

When the German was well out of earshot, Fairak asked, "How can you trust him? Suppose this is a trick? Suppose he is allied with Heiselmann against us?"

"No. He is not. I know that Dietl has suffered at the hands of Heiselmann, as we have. There is bad blood between them. Their war goes way back."

"So you say."

"So it has been looked into by our people here. I can separate the truth from lies! There is nothing going on over there that I do not know about."

Fairak Husra heaved a sigh. "Then let us hope their war does not become our war."

Fein nodded. He agreed. The vultures were gathering. Whatever lay ahead would not bode well for somebody. He only hoped the Spearhead of the Revolution survived this ordeal.

As his brother left his side, Fein muttered, "I only pray that is true, brother. God is great."

11

Château Heiselmann was his pride and joy. Whenever the German armorer entered the huge conference hall on the second floor of the château he had acquired and restored ten years earlier, he let his gaze linger for long moments on the frescoed murals. The valiant "knights" of history lived before his eyes. In color. In action. In blood, guts and carnage. Hector. Alexander the Great. Julius Caesar crossing the Channel with his Roman legions. Charlemagne, king of the Franks, being crowned Holy Roman Emperor in Rome on Christmas Day.

Then there were the darker images, images in which he saw himself as a titan doing battle against the savage hordes. The Armageddon-like struggle between the German barbarians and the bestial Asiatic flood tide of Attila at Chalons in northern France. The carnage of Agincourt. The slaughter at Waterloo. The German massacre of Governor Varus and his legions in the ill-fated Roman attempt to cross the Rhine. It was dark, bloody history, but Heiselmann believed that war was the history of man and that man was essentially a loathsome, hateful creature to be shunned at all costs.

Which was why Heiselmann would have chosen no other profession than arms dealing. It did not matter to him that men were wiping one another out of existence. They could go on killing one another just as long as he was paid first. In full. On time. His love of history and his hatred of mankind were contradictory, but he didn't care. Life was full of contradictions, and the German believed that if he was to survive in the cesspool of humanity he would have to make his own rules. And impose his will on others, wherever and whenever possible. This was the way of a leader. The way of a man among men. Someone had to make the rules, after all, didn't they?

There were leaders who shone like supernovas in human history. And then there were the wretched masses. Still, without the little man, the peasant, the peon, the collective farmer, the serf, where would the great men of history be? Heiselmann was smart enough to know he needed all the little men he could surround himself with. The inferiors of the human race should always struggle with their lives, shed their blood and sacrifice their existence to assure the place of the great man in history. If his thinking was deemed twisted, so what?

Madness, indeed, madness. Everywhere Heiselmann turned, all was madness. And the world was daily being gripped tighter in that vise of insanity. Perhaps life had been simpler in the Dark Ages, when the only things that had concerned a man had been sex, eating, drinking and riding out to battle. Now the world was run by money rather than by iron, controlled by gutless politicians rather than by wealthy landowners and their mercenary armies. There just weren't any true warriors anymore. The days when men squared off and went toe-to-toe were long dead. Had died at Stalingrad. At Sevastopol. In the Ardennes, and finally in the battle for Berlin. The world had not been right since. Nowadays these terrorists with half-baked ideas were running around killing innocent women and children, blowing up cars on crowded city streets and shooting crippled old men. It was all petty plundering. There seemed to be no room in the world anymore for guts, for glory.

Moving toward a large stained-glass window as Teuffel and Arcadi filed into the room behind him, Heiselmann turned his thoughts to another problem.

Peter Maxwell. Who was he, really? What did he want? Perhaps he was who he claimed to be. Then again, if Maxwell was an impostor...

Heiselmann recalled the report that was given to him just minutes ago, about the affair in Deuer Rochaine. Two of Teuffel's deadliest, most savage killers had been found dead. Now, he thought, unable to keep a smile from flickering over his lips, that must have been some real heady head-cracking action. One had been shot in the chest at point-blank range, the other had had half his neck ripped away.

And then there was the business of those freighters, all three of which were now resting at the bottom of the harbor, sunk by a series of powerful and mysterious explosions. But Heiselmann believed there was no mystery about it. They had been sabotaged. But why? Indeed, this Peter Maxwell had some questions to answer.

Heiselmann pushed open the window. Cold air blasted his face, but the chill that shivered through his body felt good. Long, fluffy belts of white cloud covered the granite peaks of the massive Pyrenees. It was an awesome sight. The mountains made him feel small, yet somehow majestic and powerful. The immortal Pyrenees. His ageless château. Perhaps he was meant to be a part of history. Perhaps this deal and the revolution and bloodshed and utter destruction that would follow because of it would find for him some place in world history.

For the moment, he settled for the feeling of being part of the history of his château, imagining the ghosts of French aristocracy and landowners lost out there on the slopes of the Pyrenees.

He had been told that the château had been built by a landowner sometime near the end of the Dark Ages to protect himself from the barbarians. But the German armorer found it strange that the château was set high on a ridge, almost a thousand feet above the valley. There was no country village in that valley, no sign of any ruins, not even buildings restored from the crumbling rubble of a time long dead. But perhaps, he reasoned, the barbarians had laid waste to that village, trampled flesh and stone alike into the very soil of a blood-soaked earth. With more than ten thousand châteaus in France, he knew the history of such places could be distorted or forgotten over the centuries. History was, after all, written by man or passed along by word of mouth. And who could ever trust man to get it right?

No, there was nothing on that ridge beyond the fortress wall except jagged rock and the wild goats. Suddenly he felt very empty. History was nothing more than a memory of a string of events. And memories faded with time. And time took everyone into the grave.

As Heiselmann came out of his reverie he spotted three jeeps wending their way up the rugged mountain trail. The vehicles pulled up in front of the château, and men got out. Peter Maxwell and the Frenchman were being escorted by his soldiers. *Gut.* It was time to get some answers.

Heiselmann closed the window and turned to face Teuffel and Paul Arcadi, who stood at the far end of the oak knight's table. Arcadi, he thought, Machelli's fair-haired boy. Heiselmann had never had any use for Machelli beyond getting the arms shipped across the Atlantic. He was even considering putting the Italian out of business. But, it seemed, someone else was already in the process of doing just that. And he had a feeling he knew who that someone was.

The German armorer looked pointedly at Arcadi. "Tell me about this Peter Maxwell."

Arcadi shrugged. "What's there to tell, Mr. Heiselmann? I'd never laid eyes on the dude until yesterday. But it's funny, don't you think?"

"What is so funny?" Heiselmann growled, finding nothing funny about anything at this point. Not with hundreds of millions of dollars on the line.

"That this guy would just show up out of the friggin' blue. I mean, we've all been doing business for years and know the players."

Arcadi paused, his brow furrowed.

"What is it?"

Arcadi grunted. "Well...there was this dude at the house..."

"What *dude*? Speak up, man!"

"I don't know who he was. Had one mean-looking scar that ran down the side of his face, I remember that. And eyes like chips of ice, but greenish. Hell, the frogs even acted kinda scared of him. Like some badass reputation was following the guy around."

Axeundarth. The hired killer that Bach-Zelewski had called in. And just where was Bach-Zelewski now, anyway? Heiselmann had a few questions for his East German counterpart in the terror-for-sale business, such as why Axeundarth had even been brought in at all. Rumor had it that Bach-Zelewski had put out a contract on a very big "problem." Heiselmann was not privy to the who and why of that problem, but he had to find Bach-Zelewski. The East German supposedly had gone to America to make the final arrangements for the shipment. Gone with the Frenchman. So where was he? Just what the hell was going on?

"What about this scar-faced man?"

"Well, he acted like he was in charge—"

"He was. Continue."

Arcadi faltered, his mouth hanging open for a second. "Uh, yeah... Anyway, he left the house. Said he was going to check on my guys, like they were cherry punks fresh out of a pool hall."

"So, he left the house?"

"Yeah, he left a few minutes before..."

"The attack, I see," Heiselmann finished. But the German armorer didn't see at all. Questions were piling up fast and furious, and there were no answers, not even a clue as to what was happening.

But he had an idea that might shed some light on Peter Maxwell.

"Teuffel, we need answers. However, I do not intend to be abrupt or obvious about my suspicions any longer."

"Maxwell?"

"*Ja*. Let us play him out awhile longer. We need to see him in action. Again. Only this time up close—so close you will be practically right in his face. There is a job that must be done, and you and Mr. Maxwell will take care of it. I want our competition eliminated. Point-blank. Tonight. He has become one of our biggest problems, it seems. You know who I am speaking of."

Teuffel smiled. "Dietl?"

"Exactly. The thorn in our side."

"As you mentioned to me on the way here, he has been seen with Fein Husra. Perhaps he turned the Arab on to the scent of treachery."

"My suspicions exactly. Our Mr. Maxwell is on the way up now. I have a plan. During this hit you shall be Maxwell's...guardian angel. And if anything, anything at all, appears suspicious to you about him, you shall be his angel of death."

Teuffel nodded. "Consider it done."

HEISELMANN'S SOLDIERS FLANKED Bolan and Borbambeau, leading them up the stone spiral staircase.

The eleventh hour, Bolan knew, was fast approaching. He doubted that he would be able to keep up the masquerade much longer. Not after the violence he had left behind in Deuer Rochaine.

After departing the harbor with its burning, listing deathships, Bolan had returned to the warjet. During the hours before and following the Bolan invasion of the Deuer Rochaine harbor, Grimaldi had seen no sign of Heiselmann's goons or anybody else, for that matter. Strange. Bolan didn't know whether to take the absence of gunmen near or around the jet as a good sign or an omen of a trap being laid. Whichever, both Bolan and Grimaldi had decided to forge ahead. All firepower-systems go.

The Executioner would present Heiselmann with a different story about the events in Deuer Rochaine—Machelli was dead by Peter Maxwell's own hand, and the mobster's ships had been sunk as part of a personal vendetta. The Frenchman would vouch for that. The vengeance plot had been engineered by Borbambeau in reprisal for a hit the American merchant of death had put on an associate of his about a year ago. Time and place were unimportant. Bolan would have to be as honest as possible, but evasive where necessary. It would take days, maybe even weeks, Bolan knew, for Heiselmann to have the story checked out.

By then, a hellstorm would have consumed all guilty parties.

Or Mack Bolan.

Because he had been allowed to keep Big Thunder and the Beretta 93-R leathered and by his side, the warrior was assuming that the storm was merely building on the horizon. And he hated like hell having to assume anything at this point.

Grimaldi had cleaned and stitched the deep gash in Bolan's shoulder, sterilized and bandaged the ugly cut on the side of the Executioner's neck. Another inch to the left, and that knifeman's blade would have severed his jugular. And Bolan was going to confront Heiselmann about that. As long as he was laying his own black cards out on the table, he would expect the German armorer to deal straight with him. Straight, sure. About as straight as a broken arrow.

Then there was the wild card, Paul Arcadi. Machelli's errand boy.

Mack Bolan had a plan for Machelli, an explosive plan. A grandstand play that would send everybody, himself included, teetering on the brink of disaster. And doom. It was a risk he was willing to take. No, check that. Had to take. A gamble that was going to back his story, and silence one more problem. Grimaldi was now waiting in the wings in case all hell broke loose. He had followed the tractor-trailer convoy to Heiselmann's stronghold in the warjet. Condor was grounded in the valley, a thousand feet below where the final showdown might take place.

Two of Heiselmann's soldiers opened the massive double doors at the end of the stone-corbeled hallway. As Bolan stepped into the room, he got the feeling he was under Heiselmann's personal microscope. He unzipped his black leather flight jacket. He was ready.

"Gentlemen," the German armorer greeted, nodding curtly, his hands clasped behind his back. "We have business to discuss. *Bitte*," he said, gesturing toward the chairs lined in front of the long oak table. "Sit."

Bolan pinned Arcadi with an icy stare.

"Herr Maxwell. Is something wrong?"

"Yeah," Bolan growled. "This."

The .44 AutoMag streaked away from quick-draw leather.

Everyone in the room froze.

Bolan swung the stainless-steel hand cannon toward Paul Arcadi and squeezed the trigger.

12

The 240-grain boattail blasted through Arcadi's nose. Muzzling at 1640 feet per second, the .44 revolver bullet, with its cut-down 7.62 mm NATO rifle casing, could tear through the solid metal of an automobile engine block. Paul Arcadi became instant dead proof that the .44 Magnum is, indeed, the world's most powerful handgun. One slug decapitated Machelli's muscle where he stood. Blood and brains washed over the mural of the carnage at Waterloo.

Shock paralyzed Heiselmann, Teuffel and Borbambeau.

As the report of the death message echoed through the room, Heiselmann's soldiers poured through the doorway, guns drawn and leveled at Bolan.

Balanced on the knife's edge of eternity, the warrior was a breath away from throwing himself into a roll ana coming up firing.

It was the German armorer who prevented the bloodbath. "Hold your fire!" he yelled.

Bolan thrust his hands into the air.

With rough hands, the gunmen stripped him of his weapons

Borbambeau wobbled on rubbery legs, looked set to vomit as Arcadi's headless corpse toppled to the cold stone floor.

"He had it coming," Bolan growled.

"I suggest you explain that," Heiselmann shot back.

"If you don't already know, Heiselmann, I sank Machelli's ships last night."

"Why would you say I already knew such a thing?"

"This," Bolan rasped. He reached for his jacket but felt the muzzle of a revolver jab against his spine. "You mind? I got something to show here."

Heiselmann nodded at the gunman, who lowered the revolver.

Yanking up the black wool sweater, Bolan showed Heiselmann the bandage around his shoulder.

"The one on my neck is obvious. Now you tell me, Heiselmann. Why?"

The German laughed.

"My being pissed off is funny, Heiselmann?"

"*Nein*, *nein*, certainly not, Herr Maxwell. Okay. I had you followed."

"I'd say you had more than a dogwatching in mind, guy."

"Of course," Heiselmann admitted. "I wanted you sized...sized up for action, so to speak. Perhaps even for a promotion."

Heiselmann was making less sense to Bolan by the second. Who was trying to outmasquerade whom?

"So you tried to have me killed?"

"Obviously you are more man than we have given you credit for."

Bolan wanted Borbambeau to take the cue, put on his best indignant face and launch himself into a tirade, but the man was white as a sheet. Borbambeau sat down hard in one of the straight-backed wooden chairs and braced his hands on the edge of the table. The Frenchman was shaken up bad, and Bolan feared the guy would come apart at the seams any second, blow his cover since the guns were staring "Peter Maxwell" in the face.

"I don't know what kind of game it is you're playing...."

"Perhaps, Herr Maxwell, you should explain what kind of game it is you're playing."

"A vendetta. That's no game to me. Machelli was marked. By my employer here, Mr. Borbambeau." Bolan met the Frenchman's eyes, and he nodded lamely. The man was lost in his own little world of fear, completely oblivious, it seemed, to the fact that he had been stripped of his weapons. If the Frenchman was going to sound the alarm, he'd better do it now, Bolan thought. He knew he had to get his guns back. Fast. Within seconds.

"*Oui*... *oui*. It is true. A v-vendetta."

"Was," Bolan went on, "because Machelli is dead. I iced him before we left. The contract's needed filling for some time. A mutual associate of ours was hit last year by Machelli."

"A mutual associate?"

It wasn't a question, but Bolan played it as such. "Yeah. Sinking his freighters was the finishing touch."

"So now you have inconvenienced us for all future operations because of your personal vendetta."

"Tough," Bolan said. "The big deal is going down. There'll be others, but not through Machelli."

"And who do you propose it is I now deal with?"

"Us," Bolan said. "Me. I've got a big score in the works. But I'm not giving you anything else to go, Heiselmann, until I feel I can trust you."

"That works both ways, Herr Maxwell."

"So it does."

The German appeared to think hard about what Peter Maxwell had just said. Finally he jerked a nod at the gunmen by the door, waved a hand over the corpse.

"Get this garbage out of here, and leave us," he ordered.

One by one they were going down, Bolan thought as he watched Heiselmann's goons manhandle the corpse out of the room. Hell, one by one wasn't going to be good enough.

"How about my hardware, Heiselmann?" Bolan demanded, hoping he wasn't rolling the dice for the last time. "A little show of your trust, huh? For starters."

Heiselmann frowned, but nodded at his soldiers. Reluctantly they returned Bolan's weapons.

When Arcadi's body was hauled from the room and the doors shut, Heiselmann met the Executioner's gaze for several moments.

"I am trusting you, Herr Maxwell...but only up to a point."

"I understand."

"No, you don't."

"Spit it out."

"There has been a change in plan."

"Such as?"

"The shipment will be flown out of here in one hour. Next stop: Malta. From there, the shipment and the C-130s are going to an Arab terrorist, Fein Ali Husra. He is the leader of a group of fanatics called—"

"Yeah, I know about the Spearhead of the Revolution. We can skip the briefing."

Heiselmann cleared his throat, obviously annoyed by Bolan's abruptness. "Herr Maxwell, I care nothing for this Fein Husra—he is merely a pawn in a much bigger scheme. A plan I am about to set in motion. Do you know of a man, an East German named Bach-Zelewski?"

"Wouldn't be related to Friedrich von dem, the SS general who put down the Warsaw uprising in 1944, would he?"

"I find your attempts at humor excruciatingly painful, Herr Maxwell. That whole period was a very tragic time for my people. It has not been forgotten. We were a mere few critical moves from conquering the world. We were denied our destiny by circumstances beyond our control. It will not happen this time. I am here to see that my people return to the course of their true destiny, their rightful and great place in the world and in history. Bach-Zelewski is a key figure in our half of this forthcoming revolution. He was supposed to have been at that conference in Colorado. Do you know who I mean?"

"If he was there, we didn't see him."

"Borbambeau?"

The Frenchman shook his head. "He never arrived."

Bolan felt his heart skip a beat. The Frenchman was no longer the convincing liar he had been. But Heiselmann appeared to believe him.

Heiselmann sighed. "This Spearhead of the Revolution will be used to open the gates of what will be a flood tide of new National Socialist insurgency. The underground movement on the continent has already begun. Bach-Zelewski has acquired quite a large following and stored the necessary arms. The mission is but days away from beginning."

"So what about Fein Husra?" Bolan asked. "How does he fit in?"

"He doesn't. He is something to be used. I have pilots who are prepared to fly those Arabs to the targeted cities of Eastern and Western Europe. Those cities will be razed by the Arabs manning the cannons, while their ground forces wreak terror and havoc in other targeted areas. Two other major cities will then be taken hostage. Military installations, police stations, airfields . . . they will be the first targets to be knocked out."

Bolan knew the guy was crazy. The Russians would roll right in with a sea of T-72s. Western Europe would be thrown into a state of terror and panic, and the entire world would be pushed to the brink of Armageddon. And for what? Bolan had never given much thought to World War III scenarios, but in the back of his mind he had always suspected some madman, some crackpot would be the catalyst to the beginning of the end.

"The Berlin Wall, of course, will have to be knocked out...."

Of course. And, of course, it will never work, Bolan thought. Sure, there would be a bloodbath, chaos and horror unequaled on the European continent in more than forty years.

"Bach-Zelewski's troops will also move into the hostage cities," Heiselmann continued. "And we have thousands of followers who are at this moment waiting to take up arms once the dawn of the new National Socialism breaks. Of course, we expect some casualties." The German armorer showed Bolan a sly smile. "Such as the two men you eliminated in Deuer Rochaine."

"And after that one, you expect me to think that I can trust you? That you won't want my ass?"

"As I said, we expect casualties along the way. The struggle will be a titanic one. Which brings me to another point... You and Herr Teuffel will be flying out of here in forty-five minutes. The choppers are now waiting. You see, before I can begin the master plan, I must cover my flanks and rear, so to speak."

"You want somebody taken out?"

"Exactly. A rival. An armorer himself, but one who has grown very powerful in the past few months. I should have had him taken care of years ago, but he is like a snake. He bites when cornered and hides from danger when he does not have the advantage. His name is Bernhard Dietl. My sources in North Africa have seen him with Fein Husra. They are seeking to usurp me and seize the shipment for themselves, I am certain. Dietl must be killed. His fortress will be hit tonight. I want nothing left behind but smoking rubble. Do you understand?"

"You want me fly in with your hit team and assist. Yeah, I understand. Can I make a suggestion?"

"By all means."

"You said a fortress, right?"

"Ja."

"How about letting my pilot hit the place first. An air strike. Soften the target site up."

"That is exactly what I had in mind, Herr Maxwell. You see, I have close to two hundred men here under my employ. Almost all of them will be needed to assist in the shipment from now on. You and Herr Teuffel will be taking fifty guns with you."

"Against how many?"

"You will be outnumbered two to one. I would not even have considered it but for your warjet. I am anxious to hear how it does. A thorough reconnaissance has been done of Dietl's stronghold."

"Which is where?"

"Someplace in Belgium. That is all you need to know. Go now. And good luck."

"Wait a minute," Bolan said. "There's something you'd better think about."

"Like what?"

"Fein Husra. If he's trying to double-cross you..."

"I know what you are leading up to. I intend to see the shipment delivered. I will have enough firepower on hand to discourage the Arabs from making some suicidal play at sabotage or kidnapping. Fein Husra has already agreed to assist in our plan; that was part of the arrangement. There will be no double cross here. If necessary, Fein Husra and his people will carry out their mission at gunpoint. After all," he said, smiling, "they will be dying for the glory of Allah and Islam, and their place will be assured in heaven if they are killed in battle against the infidels."

Warning bells were sounding in Bolan's head. Why did he get the feeling that he was being set up? Maybe it was the way Heiselmann looked at him—like a shark circling a piece of bloody chum.

"Oh, and Herr Borbambeau will stay here, of course."

Damn! The game was over now, without a doubt. As soon as Bolan left that room, the Frenchman would go off like a firecracker. Bolan only hoped he had time to get on the jet and get the hell en route for the Dietl strike. The charade was over. What next? He would go ahead and take out Dietl, fighting, of course, alongside Teuffel and his goons. That was the only option left. Then he would have to turn the guns on Teuffel.

Fat chance.

He was in too damn deep now. Heiselmann was taking his trump card, Borbambeau, away. This mission could well turn out to be his deathride. And if he was going down, then he was going down in only one way. Fighting the savages. Down and dirty. Tooth and claw. Gouge and rip. He would put the torch to the new National Socialism and crush Fein Husra. It didn't matter to Bolan who went down first.

"Let's go," Teuffel told Bolan.

As the Executioner and Teuffel left the room, Heiselmann turned to Borbambeau and said, "I believe we have matters to discuss."

13

The fifty-man German strike force disembarked from the eight twin-turbine exec choppers on the edge of the flat, grassy plain, Condor touching down thirty seconds behind the choppers. Bolan was in the warjet's cockpit, Teuffel looking over his shoulder.

Bolan checked his watch, trying to relate flight time to distance and get a feel for just where he was in Belgium.

Teuffel could have been reading Bolan's mind. "Central Plains, Herr Maxwell. Just south of the Meuse River." Turning his attention to Grimaldi, he said, "You will synchronize your timepiece, coordinate your strike with our attack. It will take us exactly one hour and twenty-five minutes to get there by foot. You will be accompanied by two of my men, Herr James. They will give you the orders, and their orders will come from me by radio.. Your first objective is to knock out the wall. The bulk of our forces," he told Bolan, "will go in for a frontal attack. You and I will lead a team in from the rear. Get what weapons you need. Any questions?"

Bolan shook his head.

"*Gut*. Move your ass out of here, then."

Teuffel wheeled, thrust open the door to the fuselage and left Bolan and Grimaldi alone.

"Mack."

Bolan looked at his longtime ally. There was dark concern in Grimaldi's eyes.

"If Heiselmann's got Borbambeau..."

"We're on our own, Jack. Borbambeau will talk, you can bet on it. We've stretched this thing as far as we could. I suggest we play it as it comes at us. We'll deal with Teuffel and his goons later. After the hit."

"Hey, you! American! Maxwell!"

Bolan looked through the doorway at Teuffel, who was rounding up his men. Clips were being rammed into HK-91 assault rifles, soldiers slipped into webbing, revolvers were checked, holstered.

"I thought I told you to move your ass!" Teuffel barked. "Let's go! *Schnell! Schnell!*"

As Bolan turned away from Teuffel, he heard the German grumble, "Stupid Americans. They are like children. You have to hold them by the hand."

You won't be holding my hand, pal, Bolan thought as he picked up an M-16 with attached M-203 grenade launcher. You'll be holding your head in your hands.

The Executioner slapped a 30-round clip into the M-16.

It was time for war.

Total war.

"MACK BOLAN, EH? The Executioner. Interesting."

Borbambeau, seated at the middle of the knight's table, shook his head. "I do not understand why you are finding this so difficult to believe."

"Why?" Heiselmann chuckled. But, of course, the Frenchman wouldn't understand why. The German armorer had been fooled, but he couldn't afford to let on to the man that he had been "outclassed." One rule of thumb: if the competition saw you could be outclassed once, then it could happen again. And again.

"It is just incredible, that's all," Heiselmann said. "Now I know who Bach-Zelewski put out the contract on."

"And he is still a prisoner of Bolan's pilot!"

"*Ja*, so you have told me. What you haven't told me is why you allowed yourself to go along with this game."

"But it is obvious!"

Heiselmann injected menace into his voice. "Not to me."

"My life, *monsieur*. I was afraid he would kill me. He is a madman. Like some rabid animal when it comes to a fight. If I let on to you that it was Bolan, he would have started killing people."

"Then perhaps you were wise," Heiselmann said, but thought the man was a fool. How dare this Frenchman allow Bolan to infiltrate their operation? And at such a critical time! Borbambeau should have made every effort, even sacrificed his own life before allowing Bolan to unravel this scheme of his...whatever the Executioner's intentions were to begin with! And Heiselmann could only guess that Bolan wanted those C-130s, intended to destroy them.

The man probably sought to terminate everyone involved in the transaction, from armorers to terrorists. Well, Bolan was in for a surprise. A deadly surprise. The German was not going to be outwitted again.

Those C-130s had been loaded with the armament and were en route to Malta. And they would sit there until Heiselmann was damn good and ready to deal.

And deal he would.

He would deal out death and destruction. To Fein Husra, then Bolan. He would wipe the scourge of the Executioner off the face of the earth.

And, of course, he would save this sniveling Frenchman for last. With Borbambeau dead, that would mean one less rival. There were already too many players in the game.

"Surely, Monsieur Heiselmann, you know Bolan will not return now. He knows that you will find out the truth."

"So?"

"So how do you propose to deal with him now?"

Suddenly the huge double doors behind Borbambeau opened Slowly, very slowly, the doors creaked wide.

Guntar Axeundarth, dressed in black, stood in the doorway. The German assassin smiled.

Borbambeau and Heiselmann froze, looking as if they had just seen a ghost.

"Like this. If you will listen."

"What are you—"

"Doing here?" Axeundarth said, finishing Heiselmann's sentence for him. "I have come to solve a problem. That problem is Mack Bolan. I have confronted this feared Executioner already. In Deuer Rochaine."

"So you were there when he sank those ships?" Heiselmann asked.

"Herr Heiselmann, I am everywhere. You should know that by now."

Yes, he knew that, all right. The assassin's work was well-known within arms-dealing circles. Axeundarth was a mystery man, a killer who came and went as silently as the wind. Bach-Zelewski had hired the best.

"I was there when he iced your two men," Axeundarth continued. "I was aboard one of those freighters before it went down. Bolan shot me. Here," he said, pointing to the upper left side of his chest. "He is good. And he will be your downfall...unless, of course, you listen to me. And let me proceed."

"And just what do you suggest?" Heiselmann asked.

"That you act as if nothing has happened. Bolan will return. I will be here. Not where he can see me, of course. I will deal with him. Continue as you have planned. And, by all means, take your arms and your planes to Fein Husra in Algeria."

How the hell did Axeundarth know about that? Heiselmann wondered, and felt his teeth set on edge. Unless, of course, Bach-Zelewski had talked. And, if he had talked, then he had no business disclosing details of the transaction to an outsider. Not even to Axeundarth. He was surrounded by bigmouthed amateurs, a stubborn, impatient lot who knew nothing about ethics.

"I cannot afford to play a game with Bolan. Not any longer," Heiselmann said. "You kill him outright. Or not at all."

"Herr Heiselmann," Axeundarth said, stepping into the room, tugging black leather gloves off his hands. "If I do not ice Bolan, it will not look good for future business. If I do not kill Bolan...then it will be on your head."

Heiselmann felt the anger knot his guts. "Are you threatening me?"

"Ja."

Heiselmann was astounded that Axeundarth would talk to him with such insolence, such candor. The German armorer's mouth hung open, and he stared with mounting rage at Axeundarth. A harsh reply was on the tip of his tongue. Then autofire rang out.

Screams and the chatter of weapons sounded from the courtyard.

Heiselmann and Borbambeau raced to the window.

And the German could not believe his eyes. He was witnessing a fierce battle in the courtyard.

A one-sided firefight.

The invaders were dropping straight out of the sky. Descending right out of the coal-dark blackness of night. Gliders, like giant butterflies, silently touched down in the sprawling courtyard as paratroopers landed inside the walls of the citadel. Assault rifles barked, pencil-tip flames stabbing through the murk. Machine guns blazed, black-clad troops storming out of the gliders behind the flesh-shredding fire of their fellow invaders. Incredulous, Heiselmann watched as more than thirty of his men reeled under the blistering roar of autofire, dead before they even hit the ground.

"We're being hit!" Borbambeau cried.

"How observant," Heiselmann snarled.

"But...by who? Not Fein Husra!"

"They'll be here any minute," Heiselmann rasped, his mind racing, knowing he could escape through the secret tunnel that led out of a dungeon.

Wheeling around, he discovered that Axeundarth was gone. He cursed. Had the assassin personally masterminded this attack? If he had, it didn't really matter. Because the C-130s and their cargo were gone.

The German ran toward the doorway, prepared to flee for his life. The screams of dying and horribly wounded men hammered at his back, seemed to lance through the window and walls around him. Perhaps it was cowardly to run, to seek his own personal safety at such a time. But he had been taken by complete surprise. And he intended to live another day and reap his harvest of vengeance.

Then a wall of grim-faced humanity filled the doorway in front of him. Borbambeau, his face blanched by terror, nearly ran up the German armorer's back.

Seven black-garbed figures with black greasepaint smeared across their faces trained HK-91 assault rifles on the two men.

Heiselmann was gripped by shock. The attack had happened so lightning fast...how the hell could they have gotten past his sentries inside the château so quickly?

Then he saw one of the paratroopers wipe blood from a commando knife onto his pant leg.

One of the paratroopers grinned, his white teeth flashing, ringed as they were by black greasepaint.

"Herr Dietl," the paratrooper told Heiselmann, "sends his regards." Then he laughed. "Two eyes for an eye," he added grimly.

Seven HK-91s swung toward Borbambeau, terror widening the Frenchman's eyes as he realized what was about to happen.

"No! Noooooooo!"

As if venting some sadistic urge, the HK-91s stuttered, one line of flaming muzzles chattering out instant death. A wave of 7.62 mm x 51 slugs ventilated the Frenchman, who jerked, twitched and spun in the lead hellstorm. The bullets tore his suit to crimson shreds and ripped his body apart.

The kill shots bounced off the walls of the room, echoing one unified booming retort that sounded a lingering death knell.

The Frenchman flipped over the edge of the table, slid several feet down the tabletop. Outstretched atop the table, the corpse trailed a thick line of blood behind it. A red stream spattered to the stone floor.

One of the paratroopers broke from the group, sliding a commando dagger from its sheath. He took an envelope that was tucked inside his webbing, and with the dagger pinned the envelope to the dead Frenchman's chest.

The paratroopers snatched Heiselmann out of the room.

The German armorer was speechless. He was about to protest, but knew damn good and well that it was useless.

THROUGH THE INKY BLACKNESS of night, Bolan and Teuffel led the strike force to the edge of the hill. Below them stretched Dietl's estate.

Silently the hit team fanned out along the ridge, weapons poised. With their black, greasepainted faces, they looked demonic.

Bolan and Teuffel surveyed the huge two-story stone-and-wood house. A ten-foot-high stone wall enclosed the house and grounds. There was a wide dirt road that cut through a forest to the west, led to the wrought-iron gates at the front of the estate. Beyond the gates a cobblestone driveway wended through a sprawling garden, circled a water fountain before the stone pillars of the house's foyer. Ten cars of different makes lined the driveway. Sentries toting assault rifles patrolled the estate with leashed Dobermans. Lights shone from only three windows in the entire house. Bolan counted a mere seven guards. Hardly a force strong enough to repel a stubborn attack by fifty heavily armed men.

"It looks damn near deserted," Bolan commented.

"Do not be fooled by the sight of only seven men, Maxwell," Teuffel retorted. "There is a guest house in the back—a large guest house. Once the attack starts, you will see just how many guns we face. A hundred, at least, I assure you."

Bolan raked a gaze over the gathered force around him. The commandos were grim-faced, tight-lipped.

Assault rifles, machine guns and LAWs rocket launchers held two-fisted and aimed straight ahead. They were eager, ready for action.

Across open fields, then through the forest to the north, they had jogged the entire distance—a good thirteen miles, Bolan guesstimated—in little more than an hour and a half. And not one of the commandos was winded. These guys were in shape, and they were some tough nuts.

Pros.

Teuffel even fired up a cigarette. He took two deep drags on his smoke, as if to calm some nervous tension, then flicked the cigarette away.

"In exactly five minutes the attack will begin," the German commando leader announced, checking his watch. "If possible, I want Dietl taken alive."

"I thought our orders were to level his damn house and take no prisoners," Bolan said.

"I give the orders here, Maxwell. You do as I say. Besides, regardless of what Heiselmann says at times, he means otherwise. You forget... I have known him for most of my adult life. He wants no casualties on this outing, that was why he gave the total-annihilation order. But I know he would like to have Dietl brought back."

"Why? To kick the shit out of him?"

Teuffel smiled. "Exactly. An example. A warning to others. Perhaps he will even ship pieces of Dietl to our Arab friends in North Africa."

That made sense. Twisted sense, anyway, Bolan figured. At least in the way he knew Heiselmann. The

German armorer was a cannibal who would devour friend and foe alike if it suited his purposes.

"Let's move out."

Silently, swiftly, the strike force split into two hit teams. Bolan and Teuffel led their team to the east, slipping through the outer ring of the forest that enclosed the Dietl estate.

Then, behind him to the north, Bolan heard the familiar whine. A descending shriek that was about to signal the outbreak of the assault.

Condor screamed out of the night, an avenging warbird of death.

And instant destruction.

The Bofors, the 20 mm Vulcans and the 105 mm cannon booming out hellbombs, the jet blew a gaping hole in the front wall. Debris blasted into the air on smoking, flaming tongues. A line of deafening explosions turned six cars in the driveway into twisted metal fireballs.

And, just as Teuffel had predicted, Bolan saw Dietl's soldiers flood out of the house, scrambling from around both corners of the old European-style building.

The warjet's miniguns turned a dozen of those enemy numbers into spinning, bloody sieves as the jet strafed over the grounds.

Klieg lights flashed on, and beams of bright white light fanned across the sky.

But Condor had already shrieked past the house and the stuttering muzzles of assault rifles and appeared to be sucked up into the sky as it vanished, jetting off into the gloom at Mach speed.

Bolan knew Grimaldi would be back.

And, within moments, as Bolan's killteam moved in on the guesthouse in the back, the jet returned.

Bofors and Vulcan thunder punched a maw through the back wall. Minigun lightning stabbed the darkness, ripped shadows to crimson tatters as gunmen swarmed out of the guesthouse.

As covering fire gave birth to the spearhead of their charge onto the hellgrounds, Bolan and Teuffel led a flood tide of blazing weapons through the smoke and rubble of the wall.

The top floor of the house was pulverized by heavy rocket fire. A trio of volcanic eruptions vomited into the air. Stone and wood pelted the ground around the Executioner as Bolan picked targets and cut them down with M-16 autofire.

Hideous screams lanced the darkness. Figures flopped on the grass as Teuffel's invaders surged toward the house, HK-91s and Uzis spitting death.

Bolan triggered his M-203, which belched a 40 mm grenade into the heart of six hardmen racing for the cover of a greenhouse. They never made it. A saffron flash, and human flesh, mixed with plants and the splintered wood of a trellis, rode the flaming crest of the explosion into oblivion.

As he advanced on the double French doors of the back patio, leading the left flank of the rear assault, Bolan took in the action out of the corner of his eye. More out of curiosity than anything else, he wanted to see Teuffel's troops perform in the heat of battle.

He didn't anticipate being disappointed.

And he wasn't.

Swiftly fireteams leapfrogged ahead in front of covering fire. Anything that moved in doorways, any head that popped into sight behind windows was strafed by lethal autofire. Uzis and HK-91s swept the building from left to right, exploding glass and drawing sudden sharp cries of pain.

Bolan had to assume the fireteam assigned the frontal assault was meeting with the same brutal success.

Securing temporary cover behind a brick wall at the far edge of the patio, Bolan saw two shadows spin into the doorway ahead. The Executioner sent those figures reeling into each other with a long burst of 5.56 mm tumblers.

Checking his flanks, Bolan saw one of the dead behind the wave of Teuffel's hitters rise up from the slaughtered bodies. That guy drew a bead on Teuffel's back with a large-caliber handgun.

Teuffel glanced at Bolan the instant the Executioner swung his M-16 around. Fear cut Teuffel's face, and Bolan was sure the German thought he was going to buy it right there. In a way, the warrior hated to let him down, but he was playing for bigger game, higher stakes. Like the C-130s, and Fein Husra.

Bolan drilled the resurrected soldier into the ground with a 3-round stammer from his M-16, lead tumblers chewing across the guy's chest, shattering bone, bursting heart and lungs and punching out large exit wounds through his back.

Bolan met Teuffel's gaze. He read anger and resentment in Teuffel's eyes, then begrudging gratitude.

"I owe you, Maxwell," the German growled in a loud voice through the din of battle.

"You owe me squat," Bolan grumbled under his breath.

Because of the suddenness of the blitzkrieg, Teuffel's fireteam reached the back of the house with only one casualty. And Bolan saw that guy go down under a hail of bullets before the autofire from the second-story window was silenced by LAWs projectile.

Reaching the back windows and doorways, Teuffel's hitters flanked the entrances while grenades were lobbed into the house. Explosions spewed out debris, and screams of agony split the night, men crying out eerily like horribly wounded animals.

Like bolts of lightning, Teuffel's raiders poured into the smoke of the deadly grenade blasts, firing as they swept into the house.

Grenades and LAW rocket fire—as explosions blew down walls—sent glass and wood and pulped furniture razoring through smoke-choked air, clearing the path for both of Teuffel's fireteams. They converged in the main hallway.

Bolan stepped over a half-dozen dead men on his way to the front entrance. There, Teuffel's gunmen were moving past rubble, walking over corpses with what appeared to Bolan to be total indifference to the carnage and destruction around them.

Sporadic autofire then sounded from upstairs. Pleas for mercy became long cries of pain, then death gurgles.

Bolan heard the Lear jet shrieking over the house again. A check run, as Teuffel had ordered, one last swoop to secure the perimeter behind the fireteams.

As Bolan reached the foyer, he looked past the heaped stone and fragments of wood. The front grounds were littered with the bodies of men and dogs. Flames leaped away from the crushed hulls of cars.

"Teuffel. Come quick! I think you should hear this."

Turning, Bolan saw Teuffel striding up the spiral staircase. He followed the man to the second floor.

There, a trio of gunmen were standing over one of Dietl's soldiers.

Bolan stood beside Teuffel, looked down at the wounded prisoner. The guy was down for good, Bolan knew, soon to be out of the picture forever. Blood bubbled out of the man's nose and mouth. One of his hands had been blown off at the wrist by an explosion. With the other hand, the guy tried to keep his guts from spilling out of his mutilated stomach.

For a second, Bolan was puzzled by the defiant hatred the dying man injected into his eyes. The soldier looked up at Teuffel with a twisted smile, a strangled chuckle squeezing past his lips.

"You are too late, Teuffel," the dying man wheezed, blood gushing from his mouth. "Y-you have l-lost. Dietl is not here...Heiselmann is gone...kidnapped...."

Disbelief, then anger showed in Teuffel's eyes. "What do you mean?" he snarled, kicking Dietl's soldier in the ribs. "Speak, damn you!"

"Forget it," Bolan said, looking down at the glassy stare of the corpse. "He's dead."

"Kidnapped?" Teuffel said, more to himself than anyone else, as if he were trying to comprehend what he'd just heard. Then he snapped at his men, "Torch this place. Let's go."

As Teuffel wheeled, Bolan followed him down the staircase, through the swirling smoke and out onto the front grounds.

"He wasn't lying, Teuffel," Bolan said, catching up to the German.

"Damn! How—"

"How, I don't know. Maybe Dietl figured you were coming for him and thought he'd better hit you first."

"*Nein, nein.* Bullshit! Dietl isn't good enough or strong enough to attack us and expect any chance of victory."

"Wake up, guy. Gut feeling tells me it's happened And there's a reason for it."

Teuffel stopped, turned and glared at Bolan. "What would a kidnapping accomplish?"

"The C-130s, for starters. My feeling is that Dietl's gone to Fein Husra. They're a team now, and they want you people out of the way."

Bolan looked at Teuffel for a long moment. The guy was having a tough time stomaching the possibility. Or maybe the German's arrogance wouldn't let him believe that someone like Dietl would dare make such a grandstand play.

Flames licked out of a second-story window, and wreckage burned beside the Executioner and the German, black sheets of smoke drifting across the hell-grounds.

Teuffel, Bolan thought, wishing he could read into the future. Teuffel, his enemy. About to be turned into an ally.

An unwitting ally.

But who would end up fooling who? Who would get the last laugh before the ace of spades was dealt?

Flexibility in this operation, the Executioner thought, was about to take him head-on.

Into the guns.

Headlong. Into the fire.

"If you are right," Teuffel said grimly, "then we have a war on our hands. A very big war."

He spun, walked away from Bolan.

A very big war. The understatement of the year.

Somebody's ass was grass. That much he knew.

"But who's running the lawn mower?" Bolan muttered under his breath.

He slapped a fresh 30-round clip into his M-16, checked the corpse-strewn hellzone.

Beyond the hills to the north, Condor shot across the sky.

Fire raged behind the Executioner.

14

Bernhard Dietl was having a hard time believing his good fortune. He wanted to laugh out loud, laugh right in Heiselmann's face. But he stifled the urge. Heiselmann was his prisoner and, more importantly, his ticket to destiny. And his own destiny was in his hands. There was no point in rubbing salt into an open wound.

That open wound was Heiselmann's pride.

Dietl knew he could always gloat—later. Now was the time for action. Final, decisive, brutal action.

Heiselmann had seen his glory days. But wasn't that the way of the survival of the fittest? Sooner or later the strong grew soft as they rode the memories of past accomplishments, hoping their reputation would be enough to carry them through future ordeals. That wasn't the way it worked. Particularly in his business. The younger and hungrier of the species always rose up to claim their right to glory, to bask in the shining rays of their day in the sun.

It was really a shame, Dietl thought sarcastically, that Heiselmann's sun was now blotted out by a black star.

And Dietl knew he was the black star over his rival's head.

Ach! The hell with it, he decided. He couldn't resist rubbing in a little salt.

"Would you like a drink, Herr Heiselmann?"

They were aboard Dietl's private jet somewhere over the Mediterranean, en route to the Algerian Sahara.

His hands and feet bound by rope, Heiselmann sat in a wing chair across from Dietl. With hatred burning in his eyes, the captive armorer looked at him as Dietl accepted a glass of schnapps from one of his soldiers.

"You are a very, very foolish man, Dietl."

Dietl laughed. "No, you are the fool. And have played the fool for years now. You should have never ruined my reputation in the business."

Heiselmann appeared amused. "Ruin? Hah. You ruined yourself, Dietl, by moving in on my territory."

That was true, Dietl had to admit to himself. But true only in a very minor way. After all, competition was to be expected, and the weak would always fall by the wayside. Still, their origins had been very much the same. In the beginning both of them had started out by stealing assault rifles and rocket launchers from armories across Western Europe. Like street punks they had hustled, selling to small and back then, unknown terrorist groups. But it took time, both of them had realized, to build any business. And dealing in stolen weaponry was really no different than any other business, legitimate or otherwise. A deal here, a deal there. Some capital to work with. Then . . . from small arms to heavy arms. With the right contacts and certain "in" people being bought and sold by blackmail, a pipeline had been created that stretched across Europe to Beirut to Bangkok.

But human nature, Dietl remembered, had played its own hand. Greed. Ambition. Then inevitable treachery. Yes, Heiselmann had tried to have him killed. Indeed, many of Dietl's contacts had been murdered by an unknown but supposedly topflight assassin, reputedly one of the world's deadliest, most skilled and savage killers. A German with an almost Swedish-sounding name, it was rumored. A man-beast who liked to drink the blood of his victims.

Dietl didn't care to remember the past anymore. There had been too many killings, too much money lost on deals that Heiselmann had "soured" for him.

Now was the recovery time. Dietl intended to make back his losses. And then some.

"Let me tell you something, Herr Heiselmann." Dietl paused, sipped at his schnapps. "I have lived in your shadow for too long. Indeed, I have lived in the shadow of death, fearing you would do to me what was done to some of my associates. That is no longer true. I have organized an elite corps of professionals. Need I remind you that today should have shown you just how good they are?"

"More than half of my people were not there, Dietl. Against the full force that I could gather, you would not stand a chance."

Dietl shrugged, as if agreeing with Heiselmann. "You are wrong. You are dead wrong. Your days as king of the mountain are numbered. Your men will follow in the C-130s, to Algeria, as they have been instructed. There, your reign will end. In flames. In utter ruin."

"You think my men would so blindly walk into such an obvious trap?"

Dietl chuckled. "Are you not their main source of income, Herr Heiselmann?"

The armorer hesitated, his gaze narrowing with anger.

It was the response Dietl had expected. He had Heiselmann exactly where he wanted him. Ass bent over a barrel.

"I suggest you relax. Enjoy the plane ride. We will be there shortly. And I'm certain the Husras are anxious to see you. I understand they have planned a most warm welcome reception for you."

Heiselmann's scowl faded into a stony mask of anxiety.

Dietl laughed and ordered his soldier to bring him another schnapps.

Destiny awaited Bernhard Dietl.

Soon to be the newly crowned king of the arms mountain.

HK-91s POISED TO FIRE, Teuffel and six of his commandos barged into the conference room.

Only death was there to greet them.

Bolan, cool and calm, brushed past the commandos and entered the room. He took one look at the Frenchman's outstretched corpse and breathed silent relief. Someone had taken care of a monkey wrench for him. He was thankful for occasional treachery and backstabbing among the ranks.

"Gliders," Teuffel gritted to himself, walking to the body that was laid out on the knight's table. "Paratroopers."

Believe it, guy, Bolan thought, recalling the carnage he'd seen in the courtyard, the trail of dead men he'd passed throughout the château on his way to the room. They might as well have been slain by ghosts, because they never knew what hit them. This hit had been done by the numbers. Timing the drop. Disembarkation under virtually no return fire, because Bolan could count the number of bullet holes in the gliders outside. Yeah, the commandos had been in perfect step with each other, from courtyard to conference room. A class operation. Dietl's troops were no street punks. They were trained professionals. Obviously Heiselmann had bitten off a whole hell of a lot more than he could chew. Or stomach. The German armorer's overconfidence had brought the bloody dawn of his own personal Waterloo down on his head. The little scene of slaughter here, Bolan thought, glancing at the murals depicting battles, would look good on the wall. Mighty fitting.

His rage mounting, Teuffel pulled the dagger out of the Frenchman's chest. He tore open the blood-stained envelope, read the message to himself.

"Well?" Bolan prodded.

Teuffel turned, looked at Bolan with simmering hatred. "They have taken him to their base in Algeria."

"Do you know where it is?"

"Of course I know where it is!"

"Then let's stop pissing in the wind. Let's move out."

"And just what do you propose to do, Maxwell?"

"What does that message say?"

"It says we have until 2400 tomorrow to deliver the C-130s and their cargo. Or Heiselmann will be executed."

"Well, let me ask you this. Just how loyal are you and your men to Heiselmann?"

"Just what the hell is that supposed to mean? I don't think I like what you are implying, Herr Maxwell."

"All right, all right. Don't get all bent out of shape. You're loyal to the bitter end, I can tell. Okay. So listen up and give me the floor. I've got an idea."

"What idea is this?" Teuffel rasped.

A half grin ghosted Bolan's lips. He knew they were really going to love this one.

"Have you ever heard of the Trojan horse?"

JACK GRIMALDI SAT in the cockpit of his jet, staring out at the valley of darkness.

The valley of death.

He was worried, and with damn good reason. Mack was digging the both of them deeper and deeper into a hole with the arms dealers. When the showdown finally came, there might damn well be no way out of that hole. At best there would be one—head up, and both barrels blazing.

Heiselmann, Dietl, or Fein Husra could well turn that hole into their grave.

Now there was this new development. The kidnapping of Heiselmann. What move was the big guy in combat blacksuit planning next? Teuffel, who had flown back to Château Heiselmann with both of them, seemed to be going along with the masquerade. But how much longer could that possibly last? Teuffel was too damn slick, had been around the block too many times to be kept fed a steady dose of crap.

The whole scheme was setting Grimaldi's teeth on edge. His nerves were just about frayed.

He checked his watch. Bach-Zelewski would be stirring from his induced sleep within minutes.

Then Grimaldi saw him—a dark figure standing in the night, several yards in front of the jet. The man was waving his arms. *What the hell?*

The ace pilot hit the lights, the figure recoiling for a second under the harsh glare.

"Bitte, bitte," the man implored, squinting at the cockpit, the bulletproof Plexiglas muffling his voice.

Grimaldi took a close look at the man. He was tall, broad, dark haired. In the brilliant glow of light, he clearly saw the ugly scar that jagged down the side of the man's face. A mean-looking SOB. One of Teuffel's boys?

"There has been a problem at the château," Guntar Axeundarth called out. "Please, I need to talk to you. Let me come in."

Grimaldi left the cockpit. On his way to the fuselage door, he picked up an M-16. He opened the door, the cold night air stinging his face. He lowered the ramp, instinctively checking the woods for any sign of invaders.

The forest was silent, black.

Grimaldi walked down the ramp.

And felt his legs whipped out from under him.

The ground rushed up at his face before he could react to the sudden threat of danger. His jaw hammering the turf, Grimaldi threw himself into a roll. His only thought was that Bolan was in trouble and needed him.

Then he felt the balled fist slam off his jaw like the driving force of a baseball bat. Stars exploded before his eyes. Dazed, he fought to gather his senses, fearfully aware that what he did or didn't do next could determine whether he lived or died.

Grimaldi was in no mood to die.

What he did was swing the M-16 skyward toward the scar-faced vision. It was a twisted face that seemed to delight in dealing out pain and suffering. Grimaldi wanted to blast that laughing face to bloody pulp.

But what Jack Grimaldi didn't do was turn the tide of battle in his favor.

Axeundarth plunged the heel of his boot into the pilot's guts, then hauled him off the ground as a terrible rush of air burst from the ace pilot's mouth. Then he rammed Grimaldi, facefirst, into Condor's fuselage.

And Guntar Axeundarth laughed.

Blood sprayed over the black paint job from Grimaldi's mangled nose. He slumped to his knees, dropped on his back. A loud ringing sounded in his head. Nausea welled in his stomach; he tasted blood flowing into his mouth. For a moment, Grimaldi gagged on his own blood, thinking he would suffocate as his life's juices filled his mouth.

Axeundarth loomed over him, then pinned the ace pilot to the ground with a boot against his chest.

"Bach-Zelewski, American. Where is he?"

"In hell," Grimaldi answered, defiant to the end.

Axeundarth unsheathed his Walther, aimed the silenced muzzle at Grimaldi's face. "As you shall be in two seconds, if you do not answer my question."

Grimaldi was silent.

Anger blazed into Axeundarth's eyes. He bent, digging his knee into Grimaldi's chest. Quickly Axeundarth frisked him. There were no concealed weapons on the pilot's body.

Grimaldi found it hard to believe, and stomach, what the scar-faced man did next.

With the fingers of his free hand, Axeundarth wiped some of the blood off Grimaldi's face, then licked the blood off his fingers.

"Your blood is weak, diluted. You are spineless trash like the rest of your mongrel American breed. You are powerless against me. It will do you no good to deny me. I am Death. I can take your life, if I so desire. And I am willing to give you more pain. Your silence shall mean yes to pain."

Axeundarth stood, looked down at Grimaldi with contempt. Then the German assassin kicked Grimaldi in the ribs. The pilot bit down on his cry of pain; he could at least deny this bastard the satisfaction of knowing he was suffering. The guy was a sick creep, he thought, a goddamn Nazi leftover.

A voice of outrage broke through the buzzing in Grimaldi's ears. Muffled banging. Damn it! Bach-Zelewski.

Axeundarth smiled at Grimaldi. Scooping up the discarded M-16, the German assassin bounded up the ramp and into the warjet. Inside, he walked up to the metal weapons bin. He blasted the lock off with two .32 ACP rounds from his Walther. He threw open the lid, stepped back.

An enraged Bach-Zelewski climbed out of the bin. When he saw the scar-faced shadow, he froze.

"You recognize me, comrade?"

"You? How..."

"No questions. There have been complications. Problems have arisen that need our immediate attention."

Bach-Zelewski looked around the fuselage. "Where—"

"I said no questions! What we are about to do next is for the good of the new and greater Germany. Listen to me, and do exactly as I say. I need to know how many of your men, good men, you can round up in the next eight hours. Heavily armed, and ready to kill."

Bach-Zelewski hesitated, his brow furrowing. "F-fifty, maybe sixty. Why?"

"Because we are going on a journey. I will see that the necessary transportation is arranged. Come. I will explain on the way."

Outside, Axeundarth checked the area around the jet. There was no sign of Grimaldi.

Bach-Zelewski stepped down the ramp, stood behind Axeundarth. "The pilot. You killed him?"

From the woods, outstretched on his belly, Grimaldi heard the scar-faced man say, "No. But he is as good as dead. He is of no consequence."

"And Bolan?"

"He will be taken care of. In due time. Let's go."

Strangling off the groan in his throat, Grimaldi, shaking like a leaf, lifted himself up, braced his back against a tree. His vision blurring, he watched as Bach-Zelewski and the scar-faced assassin walked away from Condor. Strutting, Grimaldi thought bitterly, like conquering warriors.

Grimaldi spit out a tooth, grimacing. His head felt as if it had been split open by the edge of a shovel. His entire face felt swollen, lopsided. His brain seemed to throb with an incredible pressure. The son of a bitch had caught him with his pants down. Grimaldi swore under his breath. He owed Scarface.

But what were those two going to do? He thought he had heard something about a journey, necessary transportation. What the hell did that mean? Where were they going?

For long moments Grimaldi watched the two Germans stride across the field. The trail to Château Heiselmann was in the opposite direction. So it was safe to assume, he thought, that they were after something else.

Spitting out a mouthful of blood, Grimaldi clambered to his feet.

15

When Bernhard Dietl stepped out of his private jet with his prisoner he felt like a victorious hero returning home from war. Behind Dietl's Lear jet, six more twin-turbine jets touched down on the long dirt runway, one right after the other.

Dietl shoved the bound Heiselmann to the rocky ground before the Husra brothers and showed Fein Husra a triumphant smile.

More than a hundred heavily armed Arabs of the Spearhead of the Revolution were gathered around the jet. Bearded and grimy, they disgusted Dietl, who considered himself a man of culture and taste. But business was business.

Fein Husra looked at Dietl. "You promised the snake, and you delivered. It is now up to us to crush the serpent before he can strike back."

Heiselmann spit, aiming a mouthful of saliva and grit near Fein's boots. "You'll be dead before the day is over."

The Husras laughed, dozens of the Arab terrorists echoing their laughter. The gorge seemed to trap the outburst, throw their harsh laughter back in Heiselmann's face.

Fein swung his HK-91 toward the kneeling Heiselmann, triggered a 3-round burst. Bullets stitched the ground in front of the German, chips of stone stinging his face. Heiselmann snarled a string of vile curses.

Exploding with rage, the elder brother fisted a handful of Heiselmann's hair and yanked his head up and back.

"We have less than twenty-four hours to find out who will live and who will die, Heiselmann," Fein rasped. "And you are in no position to dictate, negotiate, or blaspheme the sacred name of Allah. Curse me again, and you will die."

Heiselmann spit defiantly.

Fein nodded, as if he understood the German armorer's hatred completely. Smiling, he looked up at the sky. The sun, clear now of the Ahaggar mountains, was burning like a furnace down on the scorched earth of the Sahara. "It is going to be very hot today, Heiselmann. But I will make you more comfortable, yes," he said, leering down at him. "Take him," he snapped at his men. "Strip him down. And stake him out near my quarters."

"You rag-headed son of a bitch . . ."

Snarling, Fein Husra chopped Heiselmann across the jaw with the butt of his assault rifle. A half-dozen Arabs dragged Heiselmann away.

Dietl, hands clasped behind his back, grinned at Fein Husra. He decided that the Arab was crazy. Yet all Arabs were insane. To believe that their fight, that the atrocities they perpetrated on innocent civilians was part of a jihad, a holy war, was ridiculous. But Dietl knew he had to play their game. For now. Up to a certain point. Once the C-130s were there...well, there was really no telling how he would feel about Fein Husra then. Perhaps he would order his men to massacre the Arabs so that he could take the warbirds for himself and resell them. There were many ways to do business and turn a big profit.

As he looked at the sandbagged arenas of antiaircraft guns, the half-dozen machine-gun nests that covered every point on the compass around the compound, Dietl knew that a full-scale slaughter of these Arabs was quite possible. Indeed, it was very likely to happen.

"What now, Fein?"

The terrorist leader seemed outraged by Dietl's question for a second. "Now...we wait. They deliver, so there will be deaths. Many, many deaths."

As the Husra brothers walked away, Dietl felt ice shiver down his spine. Fear. He could taste it suddenly in his mouth.

The Arabs were going to have to be eliminated.

What Fein Husra didn't know was that the many dead were going to be his Arab brothers.

"I BELIEVE IT CAN WORK, Herr Maxwell."

"If I didn't think it could work, Teuffel, I wouldn't have mentioned it," Bolan growled.

Bolan, Grimaldi and Teuffel were standing at the end of a dirt runway on rocky soil along the southern coast of Malta. Since departing from southern France that morning in the warjet, Teuffel's troops following in a flying armada of various twin-turbine choppers and jets, Bolan and Teuffel had gone over the plan to free Heiselmann and annihilate the Spearhead of the Revolution. Teuffel liked the plan, but still had some reservations.

"We are counting, you understand, on a number of things happening or not happening," the German commando leader said.

As the warm sunshine beat down on the back of his neck, Bolan took a few moments to admire the three C-130s. He adjusted his dark aviator shades, the sunlight glinting sharply off the freshly painted black hulls of the gunships.

The mighty Hercules. The Herc could be used as freighter, gunship, ambulance, aerial tanker, troop carrier, paratroop carrier, search and rescuer, satellite recovery craft and mapper, among other things. But what these three Hercs would eventually be used for would be the death of thousands, perhaps tens of thousands, even hundreds of thousands of innocents. The Hercs would eventually have to be pulverized. But first Bolan had to gather all the players in this deadly web of deceit, treachery and murder.

"Such as?" Bolan inquired.

"We will be taking approximately one hundred eighteen men with us. A little more than half of us will have to be hidden safely behind the false wall of one of the Hercs. Fein Husra is certain to take us as prisoners the minute we disembark."

"So what's the problem?" Bolan prodded as Teuffel hesitated.

"The problem, Herr Maxwell, concerns the timetable. What if Fein Husra decides to execute us on the spot?"

"Buy time, dammit."

"That's easy for you to say, since you have indicated you are to be part of this, ah, Trojan horse affair. Safely tucked away behind the wall unit until you feel the time is right to strike."

"We're all part of it, Teuffel. Fein Husra is going to have to check out the armament first. The crates of small arms are going to have to be unloaded, broken open, distributed. You've got pilots for him. You die, he gets no pilots. Make that clear to him. Furthermore, it's going to take some time for you people to show him and his cronies how to man the big guns.

"If he takes you prisoner, so what? Let him. One night, guy, that's all we're going to need. If they herd half of us off as prisoners, the other half will be waiting to make their move."

Bolan glanced at Grimaldi. Jack's face was bruised and swollen, his lips cut and crusted with dried blood. He had been through hell. Sure, Teuffel had bought Grimaldi's story about the "unknown assailant." But Bolan knew it was the assassin Bach-Zelewski had hired. The guy hadn't died.

And that threw still another wild card into the deck. With Bach-Zelewski and his hired killer running loose, there was no telling where they would turn up next. Bolan's hunch was that the scar-faced assassin was laying the groundwork at this very minute for a big coup de grace. And maybe even Bach-Zelewski had his sights set on the Hercs.

Everyone seemed to be trying to cut himself in for the biggest piece of the action.

"Time's wasting," Bolan said. "Let's get your men on it, and get that wall up."

Anger flared in Teuffel's eyes. "I still give the orders here, Herr Maxwell. Until otherwise, I suggest you watch your mouth."

"C'mon, Teuffel. We don't have time to squabble over who's in charge. Look, I'm not some cherry grunt that just dropped out of the sky. You've seen me work...and besides, you wouldn't be standing here if I hadn't been there at Dietl's. Catching my drift?"

Teuffel scowled, started to say something, but seemed to think better of it.

Bolan knew he was pushing his luck. But this was no time to let someone else get the upper hand.

"I'll have my men get right on it," Teuffel finally said. Then, checking his watch, he added, "We leave here no later than 1700. Plenty of time to get to Husra's base." He wheeled, took a step away from Bolan and Grimaldi and stopped. "Oh, and Maxwell. To speed up our operation here, you and your pilot might want to help with moving the crates around so that my men can work more quickly."

Bolan threw Teuffel a mock salute. "Certainly. Anything to help the team."

When Teuffel was out of earshot, Grimaldi voiced his anxiety.

"This is crazy, Striker."

"It's been crazy, Jack. But the ball's rolling, and we just need a little more time."

"We're throwing ourselves right into the lion's den, big guy. Handing ourselves over to these butchers, signed, sealed and delivered."

"You're still on the backup team, Jack. When all hell breaks loose, you let Condor rip with everything you can throw at Husra's stronghold."

"It'll be my pleasure."

"How's your face?"

"It's been prettier. I tell ya, if I catch up to that scar-faced son of a bitch..."

"You will, you can bet on it. Wherever we're going, I know Zelewski and his hired gun will be right in our shadow."

Bolan stepped toward the Herc that would become the Trojan horse, as Teuffel's commandos filed through the fuselage doorway with blowtorches and sheet metal. "Well," Bolan said, "let's go put in an honest day's work."

GUNTAR AXEUNDARTH and Bach-Zelewski had plans of their own. All that was needed now was to put the battle-ax to the grindstone. And begin lopping off heads.

The necessary arrangements had already been made. In less than four hours, Bach-Zelewski had managed to round up fifty-two of his most devoted followers in the New Reich. A considerable sum of deutsche marks had bought the services of six West German private pilots. Those pilots were now navigating the twin-turbine jets, which were en route to the Algerian Sahara. At the moment, they were somewhere over France.

Axeundarth leaned back in his leather-cushioned seat. He intended to use this time to relax, gather his thoughts about how to proceed against the enemy, muster the inner strength that would forge him into fire and steel for the war he knew was ahead. He didn't have to worry about the reliability of the pilots of his mini-armada. No, they were being paid to obey orders and keep their mouths shut. And he knew he didn't have to worry about the fifty-two commandos in his service. They were all men who had done some sort of mercenary work in the past. Their blood, he knew, was his blood. They had the look of men who had killed many times. It was something Axeundarth had read in their eyes.

They were like a rabid wolf pack, hungry for bloodletting.

It was Bach-Zelewski that he was concerned about. The man was, after all, an East German. Which made Axeundarth wonder if Bach-Zelewski was susceptible to Marxist brainwashing. Axeundarth tried to tell himself that this didn't really matter, that the man was a fervent National Socialist and a hater of anything that even smelled of Ivan. But he had lived behind the Wall for most of his life, hadn't he? So there was no telling just where his loyalties lay. In the end, Bach-Zelewski could well betray him. When the going got tough—and Axeundarth knew that hell was just across the Mediterranean—then Bach-Zelewski could crumble from years of living in the half of the land that bore the shadow of total German defeat. The half where the German was never allowed to live down the hell of the haunting past. What with the Russians having taken half of Europe, having oppressed the peoples of those countries for decades, perhaps Bach-Zelewski's psyche was not all it should be. Perhaps he didn't truly believe in the destiny of a greater Deutschland, after all. Perhaps the East German simply didn't feel he was up to the fight when the walls came tumbling down. Perhaps he would just let the rubble descend right on top of him and go down with a fight. Perhaps...

"Why are you looking at me like that?"

Axeundarth pretended he didn't hear what Bach-Zelewski said. "Excuse me?"

"You are looking at me as if you have some doubt."

Axeundarth merely smiled. "Do you understand what it is we have to do?"

Impatience edged into Bach-Zelewski's voice. "How many times must you tell me? Yes, I understand everything exactly as you have said. We are to move in on the Arab stronghold by foot. We are to wait and watch how the battle between Fein Husra, Dietl's and Heiselmann's forces will go. While they slaughter each other, we will encircle them in a great pincer movement."

"And?"

"And we will take everything there that is of value."

Axeundarth nodded. *"Gut."*

"Like you, it is my feeling that a confrontation is inevitable between the three. Unlike you, I was not able to read the message that Dietl left pinned to the Frenchman's chest. You know the details of the rendezvous and where. I do not. I only know that the three of them are greedy, pigheaded and treacherous."

"Not to mention dangerous."

"Which is why they must perish—into the fire, as you have said."

"And you have no special feelings toward Heiselmann?"

"Should I?"

"That is your answer?"

"Look, I have done business with Heiselmann for seven years now. I have given him everything. Loyalty. Contacts. But he treats everyone but Teuffel as they were nothing more than underlings. I am tired of helping him and being seen as his whipping boy. It is a disgrace. He makes enemies out of people who should be his allies. He turns friends at one another's throat. Hah! And I should continue to be loyal to him? He only has himself to blame for the hole he has dug. I see now that it is time to abandon his sinking ship. Before he drags everyone down with him."

"This is understandable. Now I must tell you something.... You realize, of course, that I am not in this merely to kill Bolan and collect my money."

"You have already made that quite clear. Like you, I, too, am interested in the revolution."

"And a unified Germany."

"And a unified Germany," Bach-Zelewski echoed.

"There will be terror and death," Axeundarth said, his eyes widening, "on the continent like there has never been before. I hope, Bach-Zelewski, that you are up to the task that is ahead of us."

"I am. Or I would not be sitting here right now."

In his mind, Axeundarth envisioned the destruction the C-130s could wreak on the targeted cities. He saw whole cities in the Eastern Bloc as nothing but smoking rubble. Streets, whole blocks awash in seas of blackened, twisted bodies that looked like shriveled mummies. Everything, everywhere, roaring in flames. Wreckage and carnage strewn from one corner of the Bloc to the other. Surely this would be a sign to the subjugated Communist masses everywhere that Russia was no iron god of strength and wisdom. One mass unified uprising, that was all it would take. Forget Ivan's military strength. On paper he was strong. In reality he could trust no one to fight beside him. When death struck the East Bloc from above, when the siren sounded in the underground for the members of the New Reich to band together and fight, surely Ivan would be dumbfounded, confused, paralyzed. Better still, Russia could not depend on its East Bloc satellites to march with them against the flood tide of outraged humanity that was banding together in those enslaved European countries. What was Ivan going to do? Nuke half of Europe?

"Relax, comrade," Axeundarth told Bach-Zelewski. "We have the necessary men. We have the firepower. All we need to do is wait for the predators to begin preying on each other. Then, like the eagle, we will swoop down and take what we want. Long live Germany."

A strange light came to Bach-Zelewski's eyes. "Long live Germany."

Axeundarth looked at Bach-Zelewski for a moment and wondered if he was a man to rely on when Death came knocking.

He knew he was going to find out. Soon. Very soon. He was eager to fan the flames of the war he so desperately wanted.

So feverishly needed.

16

The rumble of the Herc's four Allison T-56 turboprop engines filled Bolan's ears like rolling thunder.

They were en route for Desert Base Allah. As the minutes dragged by, Bolan felt the iceball in the pit of his stomach growing harder and colder. Anticipation.

Showdown.

Annihilation.

The fiery end, Bolan knew, awaited someone in the burning wastes of the Sahara.

Teuffel had just finished giving his commandos their final briefing. Bolan had to give the guy credit—he was tough, organized in his thinking and speech, and he commanded the respect of his men. When Teuffel talked, they listened. And Bolan had no doubt that he would be fighting alongside some tough, nervy sons of bitches. Even though they were the enemy, Bolan realized he needed their firepower. There would just be too many guns to face down alone, even for a highly skilled, seasoned warrior like himself. That didn't mean the commandos who would help him hurl Fein Husra and Dietl into the abyss were going to escape their own personal doom. Hell, no. Teuffel and his hardmen were the enemy, too. And the Reaper would come for them also.

The plan was simple, straightforward. Two false walls, each approximately twenty-five feet in length, had been secured to walls of the fuselage aft. They were made of double thick strips of sheet metal and jutted out two feet. A section of the floorboard had been torn up behind the walls, and when the time came, Bolan would lead half the forty-man strike force through the trapdoor, which would take them three feet beyond the wall to another trapdoor. False walls had also been erected in the other two Hercs, but only the C-130 that Bolan was in would act as the Trojan horse. If Fein Husra questioned Teuffel about the walls, the German would tell him they were merely part of the gunships' configuration.

The plan was to wait several hours while Teuffel haggled with the terrorists over money and the return of Heiselmann. The leader of the German commandos was grimly aware they were all walking into a trap. They would be taken prisoner, that much was certain. Until Fein and his men became somewhat proficient in manning the howitzers, Teuffel knew that he and the others would have their lives spared.

But neither Bolan nor Teuffel intended the situation to reach the point of howitzer instruction.

Grimaldi was to reconnoiter the stronghold as ordered and wait until battle broke out before using Condor as air fire support. Before leaving Malta, Grimaldi had given Bolan an electronic sensor that would pinpoint the Executioner's position on the radar screen. There was no way Grimaldi wanted to cut down his longtime friend by accident during the confusion and chaos and savagery of battle.

If possible, Jack was to spare the C-130s from destruction. He was ordered to turn the Hercs into flaming wreckage only if the Arabs attempted to flee with hostaged pilots.

Dressed in combat blacksuit, which could be reversed to light brown camous for daytime desert action if the need arose, Bolan checked his watch: 2336.

The pilot's voice crackled over the intercom. "We're exactly a hundred kilometers from Desert Base Allah."

"Okay," Teuffel said, rising from the bench. "This is it. Good luck." He looked at Bolan. "I am counting on you, Maxwell."

Bolan nodded, grim-faced.

Leaping off crates, the commandos began smearing black greasepaint over their faces.

Bolan slapped a 30-round clip into his M-16, then loaded the M-203 with a 40 mm grenade. He rammed home 32-round clips into two mini-Uzis and attached six frag grenades to his webbing. Big Thunder and the Beretta 93-R were snugged into their customary places.

The Executioner steeled himself.

He was stepping into the flames of hell.

2400—JACK GRIMALDI was right on schedule. The great gravel plain of the Sahara stretched out before Condor like an endless black carpet. Two miles north, the desert was broken up by the jagged chain of the Ahaggar mountain range. A half moon and countless stars shone beyond the black volcanic plugs of rock.

Gingerly Grimaldi touched his lips with the back of his hand. He was tired, angry, and he generally felt like shit. He'd give his left arm for another shot at the bastard who'd jumped him back in France. The Styrofoam cup by his seat was full of blood and saliva, and he was still bleeding from the mouth.

"There."

Spitting into the cup, Grimaldi glanced at his watchdog, Kersten. Teuffel didn't trust him. The dark-haired, bullnecked German had been glowering suspiciously at Grimaldi off and on for the past two hours. Grimaldi would have preferred flying solo on this sortie, but Kersten did happen to know exactly where the Arab stronghold was located.

Grimaldi looked in the direction that Kersten pointed. Banking the jet to port, he flew straight at the gaping maw in the mountain range.

"Careful, fly-boy," Kersten said, his speech heavily accented. "Not too close. We don't want to alert them."

At an altitude of five thousand feet, Grimaldi made out the lights that shone from deep in the gorge.

Kersten checked his chronometer. "We have a little less than four hours before the attack is to begin."

"Roger," Grimaldi said, banking away from the mountains. "We'll be there for the fireworks, don't you worry."

He again spat into the cup.

Kersten looked at Grimaldi with feigned distaste. "A most disgusting habit. Must you?"

The pilot wanted to tell the German he was full of shit, because he knew Kersten was enjoying his pain.

"Yeah, I must."

Kersten grunted, shrugged.

A little more than five miles east, they saw the fiery wreckage of two twin-turbine jets strung out on the desert floor.

Men were scrambling away from the landing zone, and he could have sworn those men were carrying weapons.

"They can't be ours," Grimaldi said.

"They're not. I don't know who they are."

Closing to within a thousand feet of the flaming LZ, Grimaldi angled away from the group of men. Muzzle flashes stabbed the darkness to port, but Grimaldi was jetting Condor well out of their firing range. To the east he saw the floor of the desert rolling away in a series of humps. The gravel plain was giving way to the desert. Sand dunes. Great. Grimaldi was going to have to search for a suitable LZ himself.

"I sure hope those guys are the other team," Grimaldi said, wincing as pain razored through his swollen face.

"They are going for the Arab base," Kersten said. "Whoever they are, I am sure we will find out soon enough. We land and wait."

"Roger. I'm sure we will."

Kersten looked at Grimaldi, met the ace pilot's gaze. A cruel smile played at the German's lips.

"How is your face?"

Grimaldi got the feeling Kersten wanted to bust out laughing.

Grimaldi also got the feeling that he wanted to bust Kersten up.

"Your concern is touching," Grimaldi remarked dryly. "I'll survive, if that's what you want to know."

Another twisted smile. "Let's hope you are a better pilot than you are a fighter. *Ja?*"

Grimaldi sat in stony silence for a moment. Then he launched some blood for the Styrofoam cup. His aim was about three inches high, and the gummy ball spattered over Kersten's leg.

Kersten clenched his jaw, then bared his teeth in a snarl.

"Sorry about that, guy," Grimaldi said.

NVD GOGGLES OVER THEIR EYES, Axeundarth and Bach-Zelewski jogged side by side, combat boots crunching over the hard-packed gravel of the desert floor. Dressed in skintight combat black, Uzi submachine gun in hand, Axeundarth turned his head skyward. He gave the receding Lear warjet one final look and smiled to himself.

Bolan was here. The pilot, too. Axeundarth would slay them both. Hopefully with gut shots. It would be a good thing to see them die a slow and painful death.

The jet shrieked eastward, soaring off into the coal-black sky behind the assault force, vanishing beyond the burning wreckage of two of Axeundarth's jets.

He cursed to himself, thinking about the crash landing. Sound carried far in the desert. Even though they were more than five miles from the Arab stronghold, and with the mountain range acting as a sound barrier, Axeundarth feared that sentries might be positioned up and down the slopes. If they were, then the men could easily spot the flametips and see the assault force coming. If that was the case, then he knew they were headed straight into the Arab guns. So be it, he decided. They would take care of whatever problem arose.

As the cold wind carried the sound of licking flames to his ears, Axeundarth cursed the two dead pilots. Fools. They had landed too close together, worried about coming down too near the sand dunes. They were supposed to have been the best pilots money could buy. Their sudden loss of nerve was inexcusable. In his line of work, no man was entitled to a bad day.

The lead jet had hit a boulder, exploding instantly into a slick, roiling fireball that the second jet couldn't avoid. Fifteen men dead. Fifteen soldiers he could have used. No matter. The fate of those men had perhaps saved the lives of the rest of them. Indeed, the explosions had alerted the other pilots, and the fiery wreckage had lit a path by which they had been able to land safely.

It seemed disaster often paved the way for success. Axeundarth expected casualties, after all. He expected death and suffering.

Indeed, he longed to hear the cries of men horribly wounded in battle.

Then he heard it.

A faint rumble at first. To the east.

Axeundarth stopped, signaled the others to halt. As the strike force gathered around their leader, a trio of searchlights knifed the sky in the distance. The rumble then turned to rolling thunder.

The Hercs.

The first C-130 slipped into the mouth of the gorge, disappearing from Axeundarth's sight. The other gunships then made a wide circle above the ravine, obviously waiting while the first Herc landed and taxied safely to a stop.

"Let's pick up the pace!" the assassin barked, pulling ahead of the pack.

It felt good to be heading into battle. To be a German marching off to war.

This was the way he was meant to exist, Axeundarth thought. This was the only way a man should live.

On the edge.

Flirting with death.

Dealing out slaughter.

That was glory.

He intended to see the wasteland become the graveyard of his enemies. And he considered everyone outside his strike force an enemy.

To be crushed. Conquered. Vanquished.

His mind fevered by images of carnage, Axeundarth raced ahead.

17

As soon as the pilot of the Hercules shut down the engines, Teuffel opened the doorway. It was time to face the music—perhaps his own death knell, he thought with burning black bitterness.

The Husra brothers barged into the gunship.

Fein jabbed the muzzle of his Belgian FN Browning pistol into Teuffel's stomach, forcing the commando leader to back away from the door.

Every last one of the twenty-five German commandos there appeared incensed as the Arab terrorists poured into the aircraft. They moved as one body to attack, taking a half step toward Fein Husra, but froze as assault rifles swung toward them and the Palestinian shouted, "Stop! Or die!"

Like vultures descending on carrion, the Arabs stripped the commandos of their side arms.

Bernhard Dietl was smiling as he stepped through the doorway. Heiselmann's rival was flanked by two of his gunmen, each goon brandishing an HK MP-5 subgun.

Fein Husra looked at Teuffel for a moment, then laughed, long and hard. It was a moment of triumph that he was going to savor.

From behind the false wall, Bolan listened to the Arab's laughter. In the cramped confines behind the wall, he found that breathing was growing more difficult by the second. Sweat soaked his blacksuit, trickled like ice water down his back. His muscles were stiff, sore, cramping up. But he would have to remain statue-still for the next three and a half hours. At the least. A major concern for Bolan was that hell could break loose well before then.

"Welcome to Algeria," the terrorist leader said to Teuffel.

"Okay, Husra," Teuffel grated in a hard voice, "you've had your fun. We're here. Let's cut the bullshit and take care of business."

Dietl chuckled. "I like that, Herr Teuffel. So smooth and diplomatic. Allow me to show you some diplomacy of my own."

Dietl jerked a nod at his two henchmen. As if the German commandos carried the plague, the Arabs stepped away from their captives.

The HK MP-5 subguns roared on full automatic. Dietl's gunmen pumped every slug from the 30-round magazines into ten of Teuffel's commandos. Bodies spun, jerked, spasmed in death throes. Arms flailed, and flesh and blood splattered the walls of the fuselage as dead men hammered off crates.

The killers slapped fresh clips into their weapons.

Outraged by the senselessness of the killings, overcoming his initial shock over the suddenness of such brutality, Teuffel and several of his men lunged for the murderers.

The Arabs swung their assault rifles, driving the butts of their weapons into the skulls of the German commandos as if they were breaking apart rock with sledgehammers. Teuffel and his men dropped at Dietl's feet. Down but not out, the punished commandos groaned, gritted teeth.

Mack Bolan sat helpless behind the false wall, almost overpowered by rage, afraid suddenly that the Arabs might start spraying the aircraft for the sheer hell of it. It was all he could do to keep from squeezing through the trapdoor and coming out blasting. Turning his head, he sensed the fury building in the commandos beside him, felt the tension like a heat wave.

Bolan heard someone next to him rasp an obscenity under his breath.

"Shut up," Bolan whispered.

As Teuffel struggled up onto his hands and knees, Dietl kicked him in the face.

The surviving commandos behind Teuffel looked on with mixed expressions of rage and hatred. There was no fear in their eyes, only a burning desire for vengeance. One of them stepped forward, helped Teuffel to his feet.

Dietl cleared his throat and clasped his hands behind his back. "I suggest you cooperate with us. There is no use in resisting or attempting to escape. You are our prisoners, and you will be allowed to live, provided you realize that you belong to us... as nothing more than slave labor."

Teuffel wiped blood off his face with the back of his hand. Trembling with rage, he said, "Okay. So let's get on with it."

The Husras and Dietl looked at one another, surprised by Teuffel's reply.

"That's it?" Dietl asked, and chuckled. "Well, it didn't take much to knock the spirit out of you, did it?"

"Eat shit and die," Teuffel growled.

Laughing, nodding his head as if he appreciated the German commando leader's attitude, Fein Husra walked down the fuselage. When he snapped his fingers, several of his men began prying the lids off crates.

Fairak Husra's eyes widened as he looked at a crate full of Stingers.

"*Allah akhbar*, eh?" Dietl said, smiling, as he stood behind the Arab brothers. "Tickets to the promised land, wouldn't you say?"

Fein Husra ignored the gloating German. "Teuffel, round up your men. I want all these crates removed and put out on the ground. I want everything separated accordingly."

"And just how the hell are we supposed to move it all?" Teuffel rasped, letting the blood flow from the gash in his head, roll off the side of his chin.

"How else?" Fein Husra crooked a grin. "We have plenty of ropes. And we have plenty of strong Germanic muscle. If a crate is too heavy, you move everything in that crate, piece by piece, by hand. Now..."

Fein Husra fell silent as he saw his brother walk up to the section of wall that bubbled out aft.

"What is this?" Fairak asked.

"What's it look like?" Teuffel fired back.

Behind the wall, Bolan tensed, tried to not even breathe. Then came the booming sound that exploded right in front of his face. The Arab was banging the wall with the butt of his rifle.

"It's hollow! What is behind here?"

The Husra brothers turned and looked at Teuffel, who spit on the floor, impatient.

"How should I know?" he replied. "I don't build them. Ask the engineers."

The breath was locked in Bolan's throat. Sweat burned into his eyes. He had never felt so vulnerable, helpless. It wouldn't take much muzzle velocity, he knew, and even a small-caliber slug could penetrate the thin sheet metal.

He felt his guts tighten even more as the Arab on the other side began pounding the wall, moving down the full length of the false wall. If the man looked down at the floorboard he might be able to see where it had been cut away by blowtorches. And if he did...

Bolan didn't hear a sound, not even a rustle of cloth from the commandos beside him. It was a shame, he thought, that these men were going to have to die. He had already seen them in action, and they were good, the best he'd seen in quite a while. Tough. Dedicated. Unflinching under fire. But still they were the enemy. He didn't feel sorrow for them because he knew they were going to have to die. No, just some regret. It was going to be a waste of damn good warriors. Still, they were helping the viper, Heiselmann, sink his fangs into innocent, unsuspecting flesh.

And it certainly wasn't Bolan's plan to fight any longer than necessary beside the commandos. He hoped that the confusion and chaos of battle would give rise to a free-for-all.

Every man for himself.

Survival of the quickest gun. Extinction of those who just weren't tough enough to hold the wrong edge of the blade.

Bolan intended to fly away from the Algerian Sahara and leave behind an ocean of slaughtered cannibals.

That was the reason for Condor. Air fire support was going to give the Executioner all the edge he needed against the flood tide of gunmen. Somehow, he was going to have to fight all sides, savage the enemy and deceive them into turning their guns on one another. It was a challenge, and Bolan intended to meet it head-on.

He listened to the heavy silence beyond the wall.

"Let's go," Fein barked at Teuffel. "I want everything out of here. Get your men on it. You come with me."

Teuffel was led through the doorway, the muzzle of an assault rifle prodding him in the back. As he stepped outside, keeping his eyes turned away from the long strip of kleig lights along the runway, he took in the compound. Sprawling and well defended, it had antiaircraft batteries, machine-gun emplacements and barracks for terrorists-in-training. It was supposed to have become the site for training the New Reich commandos. Perhaps it would still become their haven and base of operation.

"Move, move," Husra ordered, Dietl walking beside him. "This way," he said, nodding toward his command post, more than a hundred yards south.

The rest of the German commandos were being ushered out of the other two C-130s. Cargo ramps were lowered. Heavy rope was uncoiled, cut and distributed to the Germans.

"Do not be insulted, Herr Teuffel," Dietl said, his pale lips stretching into a taunting smile. "Surely you must have realized that something like this was bound to happen. You know that every king must hand over his crown someday. It's the way of life."

"Dietl," Teuffel said, eyes fixed straight ahead, his voice low, menacing, "you can do yourself a favor. Shut up."

Dietl stiffened. "Perhaps what you are about to see will soften your disposition somewhat. You see, Heiselmann is finished. I have plans. And I can always make room for men like you, men who are good soldiers."

"If you are offering me and my men something in the way of work, I'm not accepting."

"As you wish," he said, sighing, boots crunching over the hard-packed soil as they passed sandbags piled around four .50-caliber machine guns, which were angled toward Fein Husra's command post. "If your loyalty to Heiselmann is that strong, then you will take it to the grave with you. I am offering you a way out, a way to save your own life. I suggest you consider your position."

"You kill my men," Teuffel said bitterly through clenched teeth, "and you act as if nothing has happened. How do you think I can trust you, even work for you after what I have seen?"

"It was merely a show of force, Herr Teuffel. To demonstrate to you that I am the stronger, that I am in control of men's destinies."

Teuffel laughed. "I like that. You talk like some conquering warrior. But here you are, practically walking hand in hand with that." He jerked a nod at Fein Husra, as if the Arab were a piece of trash fluttering through a ghetto. "You are a bigger fool than I thought. When this is done, what makes you think the Arabs will not kill you and your men? They already have what they want. All they need now is to have someone show them how to use it."

"And that is part of the reason why I am here," Dietl returned.

But Teuffel knew Dietl wasn't convinced. A flicker of doubt and concern showed in Dietl's eyes. No one, Teuffel knew, could be sure of anything anymore. Maxwell, damn it. It was all up to Maxwell now and his Trojan horse scheme.

Teuffel was not a religious man, but he prayed that fate, God, whatever, allowed Maxwell and the others to pull it off.

Then, closing on Fein Husra's quarters, the German saw what the Arabs had done to Heiselmann.

The armorer was spread-eagled, staked to the ground. He was naked and had been left to fry in the blazing sun of the Sahara—a sun that fired the desert with temperatures that could reach one hundred seventy degrees Fahrenheit.

"W-water... w-water..."

Teuffel stared down at the pitiful sight, and felt his rage on the verge of exploding into violent action. In the light that was cast over the compound from generator-powered floodlights, he saw the full extent of Heiselmann's torture. The man's punished body was covered in blisters, his flesh raw, as red as fire. His swollen tongue protruded from his lips, and he made a strangled gulping noise. The smell of urine bit into Teuffel's nose.

He heard one of the Arabs laugh.

"We have been giving him water all day. I do not see why he is complaining."

Teuffel's teeth sat on edge.

"Should you not cooperate, Herr Teuffel," Dietl informed him, "that could be you tomorrow morning. Should you change your mind, my offer still stands."

Dietl left the group and walked to the safety and comfort of the command post.

"W-water... w-water..."

Fein Husra thumped Teuffel on the back. "I suggest you go help your men remove our shipment."

Simmering with hate, Teuffel turned and headed back to the C-130s. He heard the splash of urine, a guttural belch of harsh laughter.

"See, he gets all the water he needs!"

Teuffel clenched his fists and forced himself to look straight ahead. Otherwise he would have turned and charged the Arab bastards—and run right into his own death.

But the time was not yet right. They would get to taste their own blood, and Teuffel would be right there: standing over them and pissing on their dead faces.

BOLAN CRACKED OPEN THE TRAPDOOR, which had been cut so that it opened away from the opposite wall. This allowed Bolan to check the fuselage, fore and aft. The cargo ramp was down, and the aircraft had been cleared of crates.

He checked the illuminated dial of his watch: 0345.

Time to go.

There was plenty of time to get the commandos into position. The antiaircraft guns and machine-gun nests were to be seized and used to mow down the Arabs and hold Dietl and his men hostage.

M-16 in hand, Bolan squeezed through the hole in the floor. Twice he rapped lightly on the other false wall, and a moment later commandos began climbing through both trapdoors. Bolan looked at the two Germans he knew as Kesling and Junax and gave them the signal. Both men, hugging HK-91s to their chests, moved to the fuselage doorway and opened the door a hair. Kesling turned to give Bolan the thumbs-up. All clear.

The Executioner led his men toward the open cargo ramp. The cold night air stung his face.

Then Bolan heard the voices, coming from around the corner at the bottom of the ramp. Two Arab voices.

The commando team crouched, slid close to the walls of the gunship. Slipping his arm through the strap of his M-16, Bolan unsheathed his Sykes-Fairbairn dagger. A soldier right behind him fisted a slim stiletto.

Bolan and his commando moved down the ramp, whirled around the corner. The two Arab guards saw the shadows at the last instant, when it was too late for them to react. The Executioner and the commando slapped open palms across the mouths of the sentries, pinned them to the hull of the Herc and plunged their daggers just below breastbones, angling up, piercing hearts.

Then they shoved the corpses aside, two other commandos dragging the dead men back inside the Herc.

Bolan stared out across the compound, which was ringed by immense walls of black rock. The mouth of the gorge was to the south, a giant yawning chasm that opened up to the gravel plain of the Sahara. The compound was laid out just as Teuffel had briefed them. Bolan gave that guy more points for preparedness. Germanic efficiency at its best. Teuffel had not left out one detail about the compound—from the length and width of the runway to the size of the barracks; from the number of Arab terrorists to the fuel and ammo depots along the north wall of the gorge; the three transport trucks to the south; the two Soviet helicopter gunships; the .50-caliber machine guns; and, of course, the deadly self-propelled, quad-barreled, 23 mm automatic cannon, the Soviet ZSU-23-4, to the northeast.

Bolan signaled his team to move out.

They knew what to do: secure the antiaircraft guns and machine-gun nests. Meanwhile, Bolan would lead a team to the barracks, free Teuffel and his men. At least, that was what they expected Peter Maxwell to do. What Bolan was going to do once the hellstorm descended was something else entirely.

The compound was silent. Bolan spotted a group of six Arabs lounging around the sandbagged .50-calibers at the extreme eastern end of the runway. The crates of weapons and shells were lined up beside the Hercs along the edge of the airstrip.

Time to move.

The warrior darted toward the crates.

The German strike force poured out of the tail end of the Hercules, fanning out to bring death to the Arabs.

Bolan checked his watch: 0351. He looked up at the stygian blackness of the Sahara sky.

Grimaldi would be there in less than nine minutes.

FROM ATOP THE RIDGE overlooking the east end of the gorge, Guntar Axeundarth lowered his infrared binoculars. He had just spotted the strike force surging out of the Hercules.

And he knew the shadow leading the assault force was Bolan. Could tell by the way the man moved, commanded himself, had knifed one of the Arab sentries. He could be none other than the Executioner.

Axeundarth was delighted with the way the night was shaping up.

Bolan and the others were going to slay the Arabs while they slept. Too bad. He would change that little plan. Now.

He would start the battle.

Sound the black siren of doom.

With a flick of his hand, Axeundarth signaled the rocket teams positioned at fifty-yard intervals along the rimrock.

He held up two fingers. Two minutes. Time enough, he knew, to get himself into position.

Axeundarth began scurrying down the gully that led to the bottom of the gorge. Bach-Zelewski followed him, leading a killteam of twenty soldiers.

Automatic grenade launchers would begin hammering the compound at any moment.

"Come, Death, come," the assassin muttered to himself.

18

Bolan slid through the night, searching for targets. The silenced Beretta 93-R found a mark.

The Arab sentry had been sleeping, perched against one of the weapons crates. For reasons Bolan didn't care to know or have the time to chew over, the sentry awoke.

It was a rude awakening.

And Bolan sent the guy back to sleep, into the eternal sleep of the dead and the damned.

The AK-47 was within easy reach of the Arab, but his fingers never touched the assault rifle. Bolan drew a bead on a startled, then horrified face, squeezed the Beretta's trigger. A whispering 9 mm slug pilled through the Arab's forehead. The man dropped without a sound.

"Allah akhbar," Kesling, moving up behind Bolan, muttered to himself. "God is great, and there will be more where that came from."

Bolan pointed ahead.

The crates were stacked two or three high. That brought them to an obvious and dangerous question. Were there more Arab sentries in between those crates?

Bolan checked the grounds. Behind him sat Dietl's armada of private jets. Nothing there. The concrete tunnels stretched fifty yards ahead, the barbed-wire obstacle course and the mock-ups of an office building and garrison. In a way, it was smart to have built the terrorist compound here. Because of the towering walls of rock, it would be difficult to find the stronghold without some hard aerial recon. In another way, the choice of sites was unwise. An invading enemy force could pound the base from the air. Or, as Bolan and his strike force intended to do, drive them back against the east wall, pin them there and annihilate them.

The warrior was amazed at the lack of activity around the compound. Apparently Dietl and his German and Arab hordes believed they had the situation under control, that they had won and now held all the cards. If they only knew how dead wrong they were.

He gave the signal. Half of his twenty-man hit team split up, began moving up the other side of the crates. HK-91s and Uzis poised to fire, they checked between the crates as they advanced.

Bolan looked at Kesling. With a wave of his hand, he indicated to the German that he should take the .50-caliber machine-gun nest at the east end of the runway. It would be a daring hundred-yard-plus dash across a stretch of no-man's-land. He had complete confidence that Kesling could make the run.

Kesling nodded that he understood.

Bolan looked toward his next immediate objective: the obstacle course and the target mock-ups. He looked at the German he knew as Steiner and nodded. Bolan, Steiner and nine other commandos would move out together.

As planned, Junax led his team up the north side of the runway. Bolan looked in that direction, saw the other arm of the pincer movement slide behind the tail end of the middle C-130. For a dangerous second, they were outlined in the runway lights. The moment passed, and Junax and his assault force melted into the shadows.

0354.

The timeline to Armageddon was winding down fast.

The hurricane of slaughter was about to sweep through this German-Arab base.

Bolan moved out.

Then the expected happened to light the fuse to all-out battle.

Bolan saw the two hunched figures crawling over the crates. The Arabs must have seen the German commandos. But the commandos hadn't yet spotted the Arabs.

The Executioner swung up his Beretta and drew target acquisition.

But it was too late.

The Arabs shouted in their native tongue, sprayed the German commandos on the other side of the crates with autofire. Shadows spun in the periphery of Bolan's vision.

Switching the mode on the Beretta, Bolan squeezed off two 3-round bursts. Muzzling at 375 meters per second, the line of 9 mm parabellum sizzlers stitched the Arabs across the chest, left to right. Assault rifles flew from their hands, and they whirled off the crates like spinning tops.

Weapons fire, though, had already sounded the alarm.

Bolan cursed, racing across open ground for the concrete tunnels. He sheathed the Beretta, opting for the full-auto punchout power of the M-16.

Lights flared on in the barracks. Doors opened. Shouts, curses ripped across the compound.

Then the sky split asunder along the ridge to the east. Bolan froze for a second. The continuous *whumping* sound was unmistakable.

Mortars.

A second later, the air whistling with the incoming bombardment, a saffron line of explosions peppered the grounds a dozen yards ahead of Bolan. He dived for cover behind a concrete tunnel as the earth behind him was pounded by explosions.

NINE ARABS with assault rifles were no match for forty enraged, very tough and very determined battle-hardened commandos.

The din of explosions and chatter of autofire splitting the night beyond the door the Arabs were crowded into, Teuffel decided to make his move. In his mind, the Germans were just a little tougher, a little smarter and overall a little better than anybody else on the face of the earth. When all else failed for the Germans, brutal arrogance always saw them through a crisis. Now was a time of crisis. Now was the perfect time for some brutal arrogance.

Teuffel ran at the gathered Arabs, left his feet for a flying dropkick. It was time to show these bastards some real Teutonic fury, he thought, time to show them just what *tough* was all about.

As he drilled the heels of his combat boots into the small of the back of his targeted Arab, Teuffel's warriors surged across the barracks. A guttural belch of pain, the wind driven from his lungs, and the Arab sentry was propelled outside, crashing to the ground in a cloud of dust.

Teuffel hit the wooden floor on his side, grunted. Rolling away from the startled Arabs, he scooped up the AK-47 discarded by his first victim and blew off the Arab's head.

Three Arabs triggered off short bursts from their HK-91s, and several German commandos reeled under the spitting leadstorm.

Teuffel swung the Soviet assault rifle like a baseball bat, a feeling of grim but utter satisfaction swelling his pride as he drove the butt of the rifle into the first enemy face he saw. Blood sprayed over Teuffel's face as his Arab victim slumped to his knees, holding his punished features, cries of agony squeezing past his lips. With all his strength, Teuffel kicked the man right on the tip of his chin with the steel-tipped toe of his boot, cracked jawbone and broke his neck.

This feels good, he thought. I'm alive and rolling. A veritable juggernaut!

Screaming at the top of his lungs, Teuffel triggered the AK-47 into three shocked Arabs. Unleashing a sizzling wall of lead, he emptied the whole 30-round magazine into them. Quickly he plucked spare clips off the bodies and rammed home a fresh mag. Turning, he saw his commandos giving full vent to their rage and hate.

What had been swarthy, bearded Arab faces just seconds ago were now only crimson pulp. *Kaffiyehs* were completely drenched in blood, and gray matter was leaking out the ears of several Arabs.

It was one gratifying sight for Teuffel's anger-and-vengeance-filled eyes.

But enough was enough.

"Let's move it! Give me cover fire over here!"

The first commandos to the doorway hauled in assault rifles.

Teuffel turned hard-eyed attention to the battle raging outside. Line after line of explosions were raking the scorched earth across the compound. He looked east and saw the ridge alive with smoke and flames, the black sky beyond the mountain range seeming to crackle open with the steady *carumph* of mortars coughing out deadly payloads. Somebody up there was pinning down his advancing forces. But why? And who the hell were they? His best bet was to find Maxwell and link up with him.

Where the runway began to curve from east to south, the four .50-caliber machine guns were flaming, spitting out big 7.62 mm flesh-shredders. Those Arabs firing the man-eaters were chewing up the hull of the lead C-130.

Junax's hitters were tied down there, to the port side of the Hercules.

Then Teuffel spotted the Husras. Directly southeast, Arabs were spilling out of the command post.

They held hostages at gunpoint, and in the flash of nearby mortar blasts, Teuffel saw that Fein Husra was fleeing with every last son of a bitch who could fly a bird out of there.

The Arabs were racing for the APCs near the mouth of the gorge.

Teuffel intended to stop them, and damn quick.

Breaking from the doorway, he ordered his troops to follow him. They cut across the room, and the commando leader sent the flimsy wooden door rocketing off its hinges with a thunderous kick. Crouching in the doorway, he spotted several figures racing behind the command post, angling for the gorge.

Teuffel and two commandos opened fire with their assault rifles. Downrange, the shadows slammed to the rocky ground under the short concentrated stream of Teutonic weapons fire.

"Kieler," Teuffel growled at a commando, "take ten men and get over to the arms depot. It goes without saying to pick up any weapons you find along the way. We've got to help Maxwell knock out that machine-gun nest. Go! Get moving! If those terrorists get to that ZSU, we're all finished."

Teuffel broke from cover. Hugging the wall of the barracks, he dashed for the gorge, the rest of his strike force right on his heels. Most of them were without weapons, but Teuffel intended to change that. Quick.

He'd be damned before he'd let those towelheaded bastards leave the fight just as things were getting heated up.

But the heat of death, he suspected, had only begun to be fanned by this night's violence.

The Armageddon showdown had arrived.

In spades.

"WHAT ARE YOU DOING, fly-boy?"

"What do you think? Just shut up and watch. You might learn something for once."

Grimaldi sent the jet, nosedown, on a strafing run to the starboard side of the grounded jets. Four jets, he thought, soon to become four pieces of flaming junk. He didn't know who had come in on those birds, but he had a good feeling he knew who the hell it was.

And one of them had to be the scar-faced bastard who'd punched his lights out.

No way in hell was Grimaldi going to let that pack of riffraff beat a hasty escape and evacuation. If they were there in the gorge, then their ass was grass and he was the lawn mower. If the tide of battle turned against those cutthroats who had advanced by foot on the mountain range, Grimaldi knew, they might turn tail and run. The ace pilot figured he'd have a surprise ready and waiting for them. A veritable Waterloo in the Sahara.

At two hundred yards from the targets and bearing down, Grimaldi cut back on Mach speed. Switching the firing controls to fully automatic, he opened up on the four jets with combined Bofors, Vulcan, howitzer and minigun fire. Four direct hits, and two of the metal birds would never soar again.

Kersten was checking his watch. "It's 0357. You have three minutes to get to the gorge! Stop wasting time on this nonsense!"

Grimaldi banked Condor, sent the warjet screaming back for one final mop-up. A mountain of fire was already boiling into the sky from the two pulverized jets. Grimaldi used those makeshift runway lights to zero in on the last two twin-turbine birds.

This time he started his strafing killrun at three hundred yards. Shells boomed away from the jet, and lightning fingers of minigun fire churned the fuselages and cockpits of the stationary targets ahead. As Grimaldi pulled away from the target zone, two more fireballs geysered skyward.

The Lear banked, shrieked toward the distinct black wall of the Ahaggar mountains. Behind the warbird, a ring of fire wavered on the barren earth.

Grimaldi resisted the urge to look back and admire his bomber-pilot skills.

FEIN HUSRA SCREAMED at his men to load the pilots into the APC. Some of his own men would leave this freefire hellzone with him. Most of the Spearhead of the Revolution would stay and fight. Fight who, he suddenly wondered, searching the rimrock high above him to the northeast. But he couldn't see anything but blazing fingers arcing out constant rocket fire. Whoever the mystery enemy was, Fein figured that he, too, wanted the gunships.

They weren't going to get those C-130s. He was taking the pilots to safety, and nobody was going to be leaving the gorge without him having something to say about it. At the moment, his men were rigging the other two APCs with high explosives. No one else was going to leave the gorge alive, as far as he was concerned.

Dietl had something to say about Fein Husra's sudden evacuation. Running up to Fein out of the night, fire sweeping across the compound behind him as mortars whistled across the sky, exploding warheads throwing the earth into a flaming, smoking whirlwind, Dietl snarled, "Where are you going?"

"To make sure these pilots are safe, that's where!" Fein yelled back at Dietl.

Suddenly lead whined off the APC's hull. Fein Husra, Dietl and the German armorer's two gunmen dived for cover behind the personnel carrier. A swarm of lead-jacketed hornets ricocheted off the ground and APCs. A rocket team of three Arabs crouched near the front of the middle rig. They hoisted RPG-7s to their shoulders, drew target acquisition on the shadows spitting fire and lead at them.

From beside the command post, Teuffel and his commandos continued hosing Fein Husra's position with roaring weapons fire. But, as if they sensed massive return fire on its way, Teuffel and his commandos bolted away from the command post.

RPG warheads streaked through the night. Downrange, the projectiles crushed the command post behind one giant meshing fireball. Fragments of wood hurtled after Teuffel and his commandos as they leaped for cover behind some boulders along the base of the south wall. The trio of explosions, though, ripped through many of the German commandos, launching their shredded bodies back into the firestorm.

"I go with you!" Dietl shouted at Fein, who became furious.

"You do not trust me?"

"No."

Husra struggled to keep his patience. "Listen, most of my men are staying behind here to fight with your commandos. We need insurance! We need these pilots safe! We can't let the enemy have them!"

"I go, or you don't go at all."

As if to emphasize his threat, Dietl's gunmen trained their Uzis on the terrorist leader.

Husra saw no choice but to give in. The fighting forces here would slaughter one another soon enough. Tomorrow, he would return to pick up the pieces. This hellzone could be sorted out, might make some kind of sense to him later. The gunships were just too important. Surely the flying battleships were the prize here to be captured, cherished. Only a fool, a reckless idiot, would damage or, worse, destroy the C-130s.

"Very well, let's go," Fein Husra growled. As if he were showing some sign of good faith to Dietl, he turned and ordered his brother to stay behind and fight with the German's commandos. Fairak, the elder Palestinian could tell, didn't care for the order. If Fairak felt he was being betrayed, he said nothing to lead his brother to believe so.

With a wave of his hand, Fairak led some twenty of his Arab brothers into the foray. Fein Husra watched as Fairak led the Islamic warriors along the base of the east wall. They were headed for the ZSU. The Soviet automatic cannon, Fein Husra hoped, would most certainly shred the enemy to pieces.

A lethal rain of lead poured over the APCs. Hearing bloodcurdling screams of pain, Fein saw his rocket team slam to the ground, the RPGs and three satchels of warheads falling beside them. Blood pumped from their chests and stomachs. This was no time, though, to tend to the wounded. They would be dead soon enough.

Fein looked Dietl square in the eye.

The German armorer smiled. "You wouldn't try to put the screws to me, would you now, hajji?"

"If you're coming, let's go," Husra rasped, grabbing the edge of the APC's bed and hauling himself inside. Safe for the moment from Teuffel's fireteam.

But Fein Husra wondered if he was about to sink into this firestorm. Sink right up to his neck, then drown.

MACK BOLAN DECIDED the time had come for him to go on his own.

The way it had to be.

The way it had been destined to be from the beginning.

Situation: critical.

Breakthrough: questionable.

The enemy: everywhere.

At least Bolan figured he had achieved one of his immediate objectives in setting the predators at one another's throats.

Hell, yeah, the cannibals were now cannibalizing each other. But Bolan was grimly aware that he would have to do more than just march in and pick the bones clean. A hell of a lot more.

He saw that the .50 calibers were keeping Junax's hit team pinned down beside the C-130 with frightening success. Kesling and his squad, though, were leapfrogging ahead, hitting the ground, firing, then advancing for any cover they could secure. Like the pros they were, Kesling's killsquad kept well away from any light, thus reducing the risk of being spotted.

But the 40 mm barrage from the east kept raining fire and smoke down on the compound. Smoke and debris were shooting into the air from every point on the compass around the stronghold. And Bolan saw a direct hit wipe out half of Kesling's ten-man squad. Bodies cartwheeled across the runway like broken dolls. Five less savages he would have to worry about terminating later, Bolan knew.

The warrior crabbed through a concrete tunnel, heard Steiner and several of the other commandos crawling behind him. In the narrow confines of the tunnel, the rustle of cloth and the scrape of assault-rifle muzzles on stone was a grating echo in Bolan's ears. Then the din of battle pounded into his head with its full fury. Reaching the end of the tunnel, Bolan gave the hellzone a quick check.

Disaster, he knew, was imminent unless the machine-gun nest was knocked out. Worse still, he saw a pack of enemy numbers pour into the other machine-gun nest at the base of the east wall. More tripod-mounted machine guns flamed heavy lead at the squads of Junax and Kesling. As combined .50-caliber fire kept those teams pinned down for several critical heartbeats, Bolan saw more of his enemies charging across a strip of no-man's-land beyond the curve in the runway. Those shadows fired assault rifles on the run. Three of those figures dropped under concentrated return fire from the Junax squad.

But Bolan knew the enemy would reach the sandbagged ZSU before any of the German commandos could stop them. Another defensive strongpoint that would have to be taken. Already the earth was trembling beneath Bolan's hands under the deafening hammer blows of the mortar barrage.

Commandos under the leadership of Junax and Kesling began unleashing rocket fire on the machine-gun emplacements. Because they might need the man-eaters later, Bolan had told them to try to keep the .50 calibers and the ZSU in one piece, if possible, and to use the LAWs only as a last resort. But hell, he knew they had run up against their last resort.

Still, the 94 mm hollow charges from belching LAWs appeared to do little, if any, damage to the machine-gun nests. As sections of the thick sandbags were swept away, dust swirled around still more rings of sandbags. One warhead exploded off the east wall, biting out a large chunk of rock but only shaking up the fireteam there for a second. All the enemy machine gunners had to do was to duck their heads, hold their breath, then come up firing.

Which was what they did. The hail of their .50-caliber machine-gun fire was so furious and concentrated that the commando rocket teams were given less than a split second to draw target acquisition. Those split seconds would soon become an eternity for the commandos with the LAWs. There was just too much lead flying around the runway.

Ahead, Bolan saw the mock office building and the flimsy wooden walls of the garrison. As he charged out of the tunnel, leaped over a strand of barbed wire, Condor made its fiery entrance.

Death from above swooped over the killzone in long lightning flashes of minigun and cannon fire.

With the German commandos breaking from cover behind him, vaulting over the coils of barbed wire, Bolan reached the corner of the building mock-up. Crouching, he slipped his arm through the M-16's strap.

The east ridge was lit up by Bofors, Vulcan and howitzer fireworks. Rubble and torn bodies sailed away from the ridge. For a moment, the enemy there was silenced by Condor's swift pummeling from the heavens.

The lull ended a heartbeat later.

Then the mortars once again streamed through the air. Three direct hits slammed into the fuel depot. Out of the corner of his eye, Bolan saw the huge fuel bins to the north boil up in tremendous volcanic eruptions. The earth seemed to breathe fire. A brilliant glow from the mountainous flames washed across the runway.

Their position clearly lit up by the blinding fiery aurora, the rocket teams of Junax and Kesling were drilled into the ground by the roaring .50-caliber man-eaters. LAWs missiles burned away from their tubes, but coasted harmlessly skyward. Bits and pieces of those commandos were smeared across the dirt runway by relentless machine-gun fire.

Bolan went to work on his own grand strategy of total annihilation.

The Executioner unslung both mini-Uzis. Little Lightning in each fist, Bolan whirled.

The looks of shock and horror on the faces of Steiner and the other commandos became their frozen death masks.

Bolan triggered both mini-Uzis, double-fisted 9 mm parabellum terror spitting twin storms of flesh-eaters. Steiner and his commandos spun, pitched to the ground, weapons flying from their hands.

Dead men tumbled into the spidery coils of barbed wire.

Condor shrieked past Bolan's position. Grimaldi scored direct hits on two of Dietl's jets at the end of the runway, a sheet of slick-looking fire raging, twisted sheets of metal lying at the end of the airstrip. Then the warjet streaked toward the heavens, nose up, clearing the west wall like a black bullet.

Score two for the best damn fighter pilot around.

Quickly the warrior slapped home a fresh 32-round clip in each mini-Uzi. He made to break from the cover of the office building, then he spotted the group of commandos racing from the barracks. Sullen captives seeking to become vicious conquerors. Since he was the lone wolf there in a pack of rabid killers, Bolan decided to throw more chaos and confusion into the firestorm.

He had to take the enemy down as they boiled up out of the night.

Condor streaked back, zeroing in on targets as Grimaldi brought the warbird down into the gorge from the west. Minigun fire ripped across the compound. Arabs bolting for the ZSU performed grotesque jigs of death, but several of them reached the cover of the sandbagged automatic-cannon emplacement. Condor, banking toward the mouth of the gorge, unleashed a salvo of cannon fire, long dragon tongues of flame spitting from the fuselage. And the machine-gun nest to the east was silenced by a series of earthshaking explosions.

Bolan brought up and triggered his M-203. One 38 mm HE round sizzled toward Kieler's group of hardmen. They had spotted Maxwell, but their beeline to Bolan only stung them with the Executioner's poison. Downrange, the high explosive ripped through the heart of the German commandos seeking to join the battle. The concussive outblow scythed shrapnel and stone through survivors. Wounded men screamed like banshees, pitching to the ground. They began crawling for the cover of the barracks.

They shouldn't have bothered. There was no saving them from the crushing deathblows along the Executioner's warpath.

Bolan was on a rampage.

The nighthitter hosed the commandos down with a long M-16 burst, chopping up flesh and cloth with thirty 5.56 mm rounds. The parched earth drank more blood. Death sucked more savages into its bloodthirsty vortex.

Grimaldi strafed the high ground to the east.

Bolan broke from cover, ramming home a fresh clip into his M-16.

A mortar barrage uprooted the office building and garrison. Somebody had spotted him, but he kept running. To stop meant to die.

Another killing swoop—the warjet screaming back from the north this time—and Condor raked the east ridge with thunderous cannon fire and minigun lightning.

Then the ZSU began pounding out a flaming streamline of 23 mm hellbombs.

Bolan jumped over a strand of barbed wire, his deathsights set on the .50-caliber crew. They hadn't spotted him on the run yet, and Bolan swiftly cut the gap to within fifty yards. He reloaded the M-203, knowing he could catch them off guard from their left flank. Then he stumbled, nose-diving into a ditch.

A deafening silence suddenly stretched across the compound. The mortar bombardment had ended. Then, through the ringing in his ears, Bolan listened to the roar of fire, the relentless stammer of assault rifles, the blistering chatter of machine guns. He looked sideways, realized that he had fallen into a trench. Two to three feet deep, the trench angled in the direction of the .50-caliber crew.

Then several things happened at once.

The ZSU automatic cannon raked the sky to the south as Condor bore down on the compound. Four three-second bursts pounded out 160 seven-ounce HE shells. The black sky turned white around Condor with wave after wave of explosions.

As he hustled down the trench, Bolan watched with grim concern. Under the threat of ground-to-air attack, Grimaldi gave Condor more speed. The warbird streaked by in a streamline of shrieking air—invisible, it seemed, for a split second, but not invincible.

Double fireballs roiled to the south.

Bolan saw the two remaining APCs disintegrate before his eyes. Booby-trapped, Bolan realized. The flaming deathbeds sent several figures whirling through a cyclone of smoke and fire.

Warheads coasted away from the rubble of the command post.

The ZSU emplacement was obliterated by a series of blasts that had their source from three directions—the high ground to the east, the command post and the Junax hit team beside the C-130.

Then the unimaginable happened: Condor was hit by a ZSU salvo.

Bolan watched in anger as the right wingtip of the jet was sheared off as it soared across a sky in flames.

"No!" the Executioner growled through clenched teeth. "Goddamn it!"

Condor rolled to the starboard side, threatened to turn over, then vanished from Bolan's sight as it swept beyond the high ground to the north.

Grimaldi was going down.

Grief, rage and black bitterness knotted Bolan's guts. He didn't have to hear the explosion to know Grimaldi was dead.

But he did.

A peal of thunder rolled in over the north wall.

The Executioner was on his own. Completely. Absolutely.

And not even the powers of heaven, hell and earth would stop him from razing this damn place.

With savage determination, Bolan closed on the machine-gun nest.

If this was to be his last stand, then he would bring the walls of this Sahara stronghold tumbling down.

The roar of .50-caliber machine guns filled Bolan's head. And the Executioner's rage burst like a dam.

19

Grimaldi absorbed the shock through his knees. He shuffled his feet, riding out the momentum of his drop, and the toe of his boot clipped a large rock. Stumbling, he pitched forward and hit the ground, his parachute draping over him like a giant wilting flower. Quickly he stripped off the chute pack, got his bearings on the drop zone.

Then he took a brief second to thank his lucky stars. Somebody, somewhere liked him.

Condor was in flames, a thousand feet away at the far end of the narrow ravine. Another beautifully crafted warjet shot down in flames, goddamn it. Well, the boys back at Stony Man could always come up with another jet. There was no assembly line of ace pilots for Striker's war.

But there sure seemed to be no end to the number of cannibals Grimaldi was going to have to face down.

Kersten chuted into the ravine, forty feet ahead of Grimaldi.

Because he had run the fateful strafe in at a little better than a thousand feet, Grimaldi had been able to maintain enough altitude for several critical moments. Time enough to jump back into the fuselage, throw on a parachute pack and get out the door after punching a special built-in emergency release button. Not enough time, though, to make sure Kersten slipped into his own chute. Tough. Grimaldi would just as soon have seen him go down with the jet.

The German was angry.

The hell with him, Grimaldi thought. Kersten was going to have to die anyway.

"Why didn't you tell me where the parachute was, you fucking idiot?" Kersten yelled, hands fumbling to unsling his HK-91.

Grimaldi quickly slid the M-16 off his shoulder and drew a bead on Kersten's face. The pilot saw the fear cut the man's features as he squeezed the trigger.

Grimaldi pumped a 5.56 mm window through Kersten's forehead. The man twisted to the side, teeth gritted with dying rage that stayed strangled in his throat. As the German thudded to the ground, he triggered a 3-round burst skyward in his death throes.

Grimaldi plucked the HK-91 out of the dead man's hand, stripped the body of a commando knife and three spare clips for the assault rifle. "Is that tough enough for you, guy?" Grimaldi looked down at the twisted mask of pain and shock.

Then he looked up the steep, rocky slope. Had he landed another twenty or thirty feet that way, he might have been impaled on the jagged fingers of rock that broke up the incline.

It was going to be a tough hike to the top.

Two assault rifles and a commando knife weren't much in the way of killpower for the battle he knew was raging in the gorge beyond the rise.

But they would do.

For now.

Whatever dead men he came across, he would just pick them clean of the firepower they no longer needed.

Because Mack Bolan needed him.

Grimaldi began climbing the slope.

The ace pilot had some idea of what he would find beyond the rise, some idea of what he would be stepping into.

The bowels of hell.

Jack Grimaldi had no idea that the flames of hell would grow hotter before the sun rose over the Algerian Sahara.

TEUFFEL THOUGHT that the tide of battle would turn his way with the help of the deadly cannon-and-minigun fire from the warbird. After he and two of his commandos had scooped up the discarded RPG-7s near the armored personnel carriers and secured cover behind the boulders near the rubble of the command post, the two APCs had gone up in a thundering whoosh of flames.

That deathtrap had ripped to bloody rags most of his men. He cursed Fein Husra and his cronies for being sneaky, chickenshit sons of bitches. How many of his men were dead now, good men? Hell, he didn't know, but he cared, because for each German who died here three Arabs would have to die.

Teuffel wanted to spill more Arab blood. Buckets of blood. Rivers of blood.

He wanted two eyes for an eye.

As Heiselmann often said—and Teuffel agreed absolutely with him on this—the Arabs were nothing more than mongrel Jews, after all. Yes, Germans had died here by the treacherous hands of these mongrels. And even if he had to walk down the streets of Beirut and Damascus, Teuffel was going to blast the guts out of some of those dogs.

But there had been no time for him to take a body count, so he set his mind to butchering anything that even smelled Arab. With pinpoint rocket fire, venting more rage and hatred for the treacherous Arabs and Dietl's turncoat bastards, he had helped knock out the ABC automatic cannon battery. That ABC emplacement had just been within the RPG's three-hundred-yard range. Teuffel's first choice had been the .50-caliber machine-gun nest, but he realized he needed the air fire support that Herr James could throw into the freefire zone. The automatic cannons could knock James out of the sky.

And had.

James had gone down. In flames.

And now the battle was still at a full pitch of murderous fury.

"Keep me covered!" Teuffel yelled at his remaining men, bolting from around the boulder. His men knew what that meant. They were to fire only if bullets threatened to chop Teuffel up into bloody meat. Exposed to potentially lethal enemy fire, the commando leader didn't need his men to draw attention to him by throwing everything they had into the fight and alerting the enemy to his position. This was the time to rescue the big man.

Belly flopping to the ground, he crabbed through the smoke and swirling grit, gnashed his teeth as his knees and elbows dug into the jagged debris of the command post.

Heiselmann. Teuffel's boss was still staked to the ground, ten yards or so beyond the command post wreckage. In the heat of the battle, Teuffel had forgotten all about him. He figured he must be crazy for going after Heiselmann like this, because the big man could damn well be dead, and he could get his ass shot off for nothing. Still, Heiselmann was the reason they were there in the first place. And the armorer paid his salary. A damn good salary at that. If Heiselmann died, then Teuffel might as well cash in his chips, too. What the hell would he do, anyway, when he returned to Europe after this mess if his meal ticket was iced here? Go back to breaking legs for loan sharks? A contract killing here and there? Forget that. Heiselmann had paid him well over the years. And the job hadn't been all that tough.

Until now.

This was tough. Blood tough. And Teuffel had to admit he was loving it. Every explosion. Every howl of agony. Every whizzing bullet and whining ricochet. Even the web of deceit and treachery the warring factions had woven around one another held an intense excitement for him. This was the kind of heady, sinister stuff that had made the Third Reich immortal in the pages of history books.

Teuffel had seen plenty of death and suffering, knocked off more men than he could remember, been caught in more firefights than he cared to remember. And he had the scars to prove it.

Physically he didn't think there was a man alive he couldn't take in a fair fight. He had that mental toughness, too. And, of course, German pride. It was going to look good if he walked away from this one victorious. He had walked into the eye of the firestorm, he could later boast to Heiselmann or any other prospective employer, and lived to tell about it.

First he had to walk away from it. He could savor the taste of victory champagne later. Now was the time to taste blood, deal out death like a scorpion's poisonous sting.

Rolling off the rubble, AK-47 swinging up in his hands and searching for targets, he ran toward Heiselmann. Teuffel gave the hellgrounds a scathing once-over. The battle now seemed confined to the east and the north. There, the warring factions were hurling lead at each other nonstop. Whoever had attacked the compound from the high ground to the east was gone—at least for the moment. Even though James had given that ridge a couple of good killing strafes, there were a lot of nooks, crevices and gullies in which a man could hide. Teuffel had a gut feeling that the mystery enemy had lost some of their numbers, but that they were now regrouping.

As he crouched over Heiselmann, Teuffel unsheathed the knife he had stripped off a dead Arab.

Heiselmann was still alive. Barely.

Teuffel sliced through the ropes with the Arab fighting knife.

Heiselmann's sun-cracked lips slit open. "Maxwell... Maxwell..."

"He's here. What about him?" Teuffel asked, sensing that his employer was desperately trying to tell him something important.

"Bolan... He's Mack Bolan... the Executioner.... We've been tricked."

Dammit! Teuffel knew there had been something suspicious about Maxwell all along. It made sense. Too much sense. This revelation...Bolan... Sure, the name rang a bell. Mack Bolan was a name, hell, a plague well-known within their circles. For years they had expected the shadow of this Executioner to darken the thunderclouds of violence over their heads.

And he was here, had set them all at one another's throats like starving wild animals.

Teuffel gave the killing zone a sweeping search. Fire. Wreckage. Dead bodies strewed everywhere. Shadows dancing near licking flametips, assault rifles and subguns blazing. Bodies toppling in death throes.

And the Arabs' machine-gun nest.

Then Teuffel spotted the shadows hugging the base of the east wall. They were hopping over boulders, scurrying, it seemed, for some objective. That objective appeared to be a crevice in the wall. A cave. No *kaffiyehs* in that direction, either. Dietl's men were fleeing the war zone. Teuffel had to stop them.

He looked back at his men. "Move it out!"

He pointed east, and his commandos broke from cover. They fired on the run, moving in a skirmish line.

The time had come to take the fight to the enemy.

All enemies.

And the Executioner was at the top of Teuffel's hit list.

Teuffel hauled Heiselmann to his feet, then gave the compound one last search for Bolan. Looking toward the .50-caliber machine-gun nest, he saw a figure lurch out of a trench. It was Bolan. He hurled something at the .50-caliber weapon.

Even at a hundred yards' distance, the tall, swiftly moving figure of the Executioner was unmistakable.

Teuffel dragged Heiselmann over the jagged zone of destruction.

He wanted Bolan.

All for himself.

THE MK-2 SERVED ITS PURPOSE for Bolan. The shrapnel blast scythed through four of the eight Arabs in the wide, circular machine-gun nest. The explosion stunned the survivors into a split-second paralysis.

Time enough for the Executioner to vault over the sandbags. Time enough to mop up the last obvious Arab defensive strongpoint.

Landing on his feet, Bolan ripped loose with his M-16. The smell of blood and smoke in his nose, Bolan sprayed the enemy with three concentrated 3-round bursts. Lead-jacketed 5.56 mm hornets *thwacked* a tattered crimson line over the chests of the startled Arabs. Screams of pain, pleas for mercy died in their throats.

Bolan got his bearings on the killzone. A whirlwind of fire and smoke engulfed the compound. The dead, the dying and the damned littered the floor of the gorge. Still, the enemy was scrambling for cover or trying to gain a killing position on each other. To the south, Bolan saw Teuffel and his goons advancing on Dietl's hardmen and a group of surviving Arabs along the east wall. To the west, the survivors of the Kesling and Junax hit squads were now racing for the machine-gun nest. Weapons poised, those German hitters checked the killing field, leaping over the dead.

And Bolan knew that they felt victory was now theirs for the taking. Sweet, savage vengeance.

How wrong they were, Bolan thought as he checked the belted .50 calibers. Those pointing due west and north had been closest to the center of the frag blast and were now just twisted, useless scrap.

But the big flesh-eaters aimed south and east were undamaged. Ready for slaughter.

"Maxwell! Herr Maxwell!" Junax called out, leading his depleted squad of hardmen on the run toward the machine-gun emplacement.

"Over here!" Bolan called back, waving over the sandbags at Junax and Kesling.

They came to within twenty yards. Certain now that the enemy was dead, they ran together in a tight formation. A close-knit pack of wolves, and Bolan was steeled to throw them raw meat.

Hurl raw death right down their throats.

Bolan manned the .50-caliber machine gun, listened to the chatter of autofire to the east as Teuffel's hit team chased their turncoat comrades down the wall of the gorge. A full-scale firefight was in blazing fury there.

"Kesling! Junax! No! It's Bolan!"

Before Teuffel's screamed warning had time to register with Kesling and Junax, the Executioner cut loose with the machine gun. Big man-eating shells roared away from the flaming, smoking muzzle. Bolan worked his field of fire from left to right and back again, long sweeping bursts that mowed down the survivors of those hit teams like a scythe through wheat.

As bodies whirled and slammed to the earth, Bolan instantly swiveled the big gun on its tripod. Teuffel, he saw, was crouched in the mouth of the gorge. The German commando leader shoved the naked body of Heiselmann to the ground, hit a combat crouch and hoisted an RPG-7 to his shoulder.

Bolan's line of fire raked across the hellzone.

Downrange, the Executioner's leadstorm found its prime target. Had Bolan not struck at that moment, Teuffel would have blown him out of the machine-gun nest. The .50-caliber weapon hammered out a fusillade that drove Teuffel into the ground, chewing the cloth and flesh off his spasming frame, the slugs pulping his body, crucifying him to the earth for a frozen second. As fate would have it, Teuffel's death throes triggered the RPG-7. The warhead coasted east on a true line.

A line that was true to more death and destruction.

The projectile erupted in the heart of Teuffel's own killing party.

Bolan turned his deathsights on the fleeing Arabs and Dietl's goons. Swinging the big gun east, Bolan triggered a thunderstorm, spent casings twirling around his grim face. The weapon bucking in his big fists, Bolan hosed the retreating enemy with head-bursting, chest-goring messages of doom.

Then, through the drifting clouds of smoke, Bolan saw survivors of his blitz scrambling through a narrow opening in the east wall. Three, four, then six enemy soldiers vanished from his sight.

Bolan squeezed the machine gun's trigger. Nothing. The thing had jammed at a critical moment.

Unsheathing Big Thunder, Bolan sighted down the stainless-steel hand cannon. The snakes were sliding out of the den, and he needed a viper to tell him the way through that cave. He should have figured the Husra brothers and their German suppliers wouldn't have built a castle of sand here. When the winds of death came blowing for them, they wanted to make damn good and sure they were ready to snake out of a firestorm.

If he had to, Bolan would hunt them down, one by one—crush them into the parched gravel of one of the most brutal, unforgiving places on the face of the earth.

One squeeze of the AutoMag's trigger, and Bolan drilled a 240-grain boattail pulverizer through an Arab's thigh. The man hammered to the ground as if he'd been hit by a runaway locomotive. Screaming, the Arab writhed in a cloud of dust that his thrashing body kicked up.

But Teuffel's gunners weren't finished with Bolan yet.

Slugs thunking into the sandbags beside him, Bolan hit a crouch, darted for the other .50-caliber still intact and operating. Manhandling the big gun, the Executioner opened up with a barrage of shells directed at the position of those commandos.

He didn't have to bother.

Warheads sizzled out of the blackness from somewhere up a gully in the gorge to the southeast. Autofire added overkill to the blasts that churned the rest of Teuffel's commandos into vulture meat.

An eerie silence then hung over the killing field. The roar of fire, the banshee wail of the wounded Arab lancing into Bolan's ears, he swung the .50's muzzle toward the high ground. No movement, no flash of automatic weapons fire from there.

Again, the mystery enemy had struck like a phantom, and the night seemed to swallow those killers up as if they owned the darkness.

Bolan's gut instinct told him there was no mystery enemy there. It was Bach-Zelewski and his hired killer.

Then Bolan heard the pitiful moans of the wounded, coming from several directions—long cries that raked the air.

He surveyed the slaughter. A rough guesstimate for a body count was somewhere around a good hundred-plus men. And whoever had survived this battle would not live past the first light of dawn.

Then Bolan aimed the machine gun at one wounded animal who wouldn't even last that long.

Stark naked, Heiselmann rolled onto his side. With trembling hands, he reached for an HK-91.

Bolan triggered the .50-caliber, rode the mighty recoil for several seconds. The flesh-shredder chewed

Heiselmann to bloody pulp. For that guy, the war was over.

AutoMag fisted in his right hand, Little Lightning in his left, Bolan vaulted over the sandbags. He couldn't stay there, let the unseen enemy pull him down. One well-placed warhead, and he would be checking out. Besides, if the invisible enemy had wanted to kill him, he, they, whoever would have attempted a killstrike by now.

Combat senses electrified, adrenaline burning through his veins, Bolan ran toward his wounded prisoner. Heading into no-man's-land, Bolan expected autofire or warheads to rain down on him.

Nothing fired his way. He wasn't disappointed, just a little surprised. The men on the high ground were playing a game with him, wanted to save him for last. So be it. Bolan could play the black dice crapshoot too.

The warrior loomed over the downed Arab and pinned him to the bloody earth with an ice-cold stare.

"The cave," Bolan growled, sighting down the AutoMag at the Arab's contorted face of agony. "Where does it go? And how far?"

"If... I tell you... you must spare my life...."

"If you don't tell me, you die anyway. My way is quick and painless. Your way will give you a bitter taste of what to expect in the next life."

The Arab briefly chewed over his options. Then he realized he had none. He had gone down in battle, would die in the name of Allah in the jihad.

"You played hardball, but you struck out."

Hand clasped over his mutilated leg, the Arab spit in defiant hatred. But he seemed resigned to the inevitable.

"It leads to a ravine...a mile...a mile and a half..."

Bolan squeezed the trigger. Big Thunder bucked once, spit out a decapitating 240-grain round.

Slapping a fresh 30-round clip into his M-16, sheathing Big Thunder, Bolan stepped toward the dark maw of the cave.

The war, he knew, was far from over.

Bolan pulled the NVD goggles from his webbing.

M-16 poised to kill, the Executioner moved into the cave.

20

Guntar Axeundarth led his strike force into the gorge. It was an incredible, awe-inspiring sight for the German assassin to behold. Indeed, it was breathtaking. He sucked in the smell of death through his nose. It was good. A sweet, sweet scent. Lovely, truly lovely.

Dawn had broken across the sky east of the jagged plugs of towering black rock, and a grayish light now stretched over the slaughterfield.

The massacre that stretched before Axeundarth was like something out of his wildest, most exciting dreams.

An arena of death.

Slowly, drinking in the sight of death, destruction, fire and mutilated bodies, Axeundarth stepped through the maw of the gorge. Black pillars of smoke curled away from wooden structures that had been pulped into kindling during the rage of the death struggle. Fires still crackled from the wreckage of jet planes and the APCs, though now considerably less intense.

Axeundarth knew he had nothing to fear as he moved into the valley of death. The dead were just that. Bolan was gone. And he was there for no other reason than to determine how Bolan had escaped the killzone. And, of course, to feed his lust for the sight of such beautiful carnage. Behold, he thought, his eyes glinting in the firelight as he raked a narrowed gaze over the massacre, I am the Lord of Death and Destruction. You were unworthy subjects in this mortal struggle. You perished through your own weakness. You did not deserve to live.

Seventeen soldiers, four pilots and Bach-Zelewski were all that was left of Axeundarth's killing party. The black-camoued Lear jet had done an admirable job, Axeundarth grudgingly admitted, in pinpointing their positions along the rimrock and blasting off a good number of his men.

The surviving soldiers now fanned out to inspect the aftermath of the initial battle.

Bach-Zelewski, an HK-91 held low by his side, an XM-174 automatic grenade launcher slung over his shoulder, moved up behind Axeundarth.

The stench of blood, smoke, burning fuel and roasting flesh was carried to the two Germans on a moaning wind that stirred dustballs all over the dead zone.

A grim smile touched Bach-Zelewski's lips. "Incredible, isn't it?"

Axeundarth looked sideways at Bach-Zelewski. "Yes. Incredible. Perhaps," he said, his voice quiet, solemn, as his mind flipped through the pages of Dark Ages history, "perhaps this was what Chalons or Adrianople looked like. The Vandals, the Goths, the Teutons, the Franks. Perhaps even we were—"

Axeundarth caught himself. He believed in reincarnation, but he thought Bach-Zelewski might find him strange if he shared such a thought with him. It was best at times to keep silent on such matters.

"That we were what? There? That we were one of them?"

Axeundarth said nothing. Of course they were there, idiot, he thought. They were direct descendants of the barbarian tribes, after all. Yes, it was good to be German. He would not have wanted to be anything else.

Then Axeundarth's attention was caught by his soldiers toward the east end of the gorge. He knew they weren't *his* soldiers, that these commandos were part of Bach-Zelewski's organization. But he never thought of anything or anybody belonging to anyone other than him.

"We have wounded over here," one of the commandos told Axeundarth and Bach-Zelewski.

"Look!"

A second commando alerted Axeundarth to the presence of a cave. So that was how Bolan had escaped. Before the battle had erupted several hours ago, Axeundarth had given explicit orders that Bolan was not to be killed. Even when the Executioner had reached the machine-gun nest and turned the guns on the commandos under Teuffel and Dietl, Axeundarth had again emphasized his stern directive. To disobey the order would have meant death.

The assassin had wanted Bolan to be the last survivor. He had intended to play with him for a while before killing him. There was no way he could have known that Bolan would escape through a tunnel that led out of the gorge.

Slipping his arm through the Uzi's strap, Axeundarth walked toward the wounded Arabs. He unleathered his Walther and removed the silencer. He needed no prisoners. He needed no wounded on his hands. They were baggage. They were the losers, and their fate had been sealed by their lack of strength in the fiery eye of battle. No one was going to leave that gorge alive.

"Check the grounds for other wounded," Axeundarth told his commandos. "I want no one left alive here." He looked toward the wavering wall of fire that had been the fuel depot, far to the northwest. There was one building that had been left standing. Axeundarth pointed toward that building with his gun hand. "See if that is the armory. Take what is necessary to complete our task here. See if there is any water to be found, too. Quickly!"

To his pleasure, the assassin discovered that five Arabs had survived the battle. They were all horribly wounded, and soon, he knew, they would die from loss of blood. Axeundarth helped them on their journey into death. He pumped 7.65 mm rounds into the heads of four of the five men. The last Arab was trying to push his guts back into his stomach.

Axeundarth smiled down at Fairak Husra for a moment. Then he knelt beside him. Blood, the German assassin thought. He craved the taste of blood on his lips.

Horror froze the look of pain on Husra's face as the German placed the palm of his hand on the hideous wound. He screamed when Axeundarth dug his fingers into the gushing, cavernous opening.

Bach-Zelewski stood behind Axeundarth. The East German paled at what he saw next.

Axeundarth lifted a blood-slick hand to his mouth. With the tip of his tongue, he licked the blood off his fingers.

Husra made a strangled gasping noise, as if he were going to vomit. There was nothing, though, in his stomach to release. Blood poured out of his mouth.

"You have the true blood of Islamic swine," Axeundarth told the dying man. Then he stood. "So long," he told the doomed Arab, smiling.

Low laughter rumbled from the German's throat.

With a mighty stomp of his boot heel, he crushed Husra's face.

Autofire rang out.

Snapping his head sideways, Axeundarth saw three commandos firing across the compound. The pilots were running toward the twin-turbine jets. One of the men hit the ground as slugs ripped into his leg. The other three grabbed their wounded comrade and began to haul him toward the nearest jet.

"Stop! Hold your fire!" Axeundarth yelled.

The commandos looked at him, surprised.

"Let them go."

"They are escaping," Bach-Zelewski protested. "They are our only means out of here."

Axeundarth ignored Bach-Zelewski.

Holstering his Walther, he checked the immediate area around him and found what he was looking for.

Axeundarth slid a gold case from his webbing. From the case he pulled out an Upmann and fired up the cigar with his lighter. He took a deep drag. The taste of blood and acrid cigar smoke sent a tingle down his spine.

The assassin walked away from the east wall. Moments later, he picked up an RPG-7 and armed the Russian rocket launcher with an 85 mm warhead. He slung the satchel stuffed with projectiles over his shoulder. Slowly he walked toward the runway.

The twin-turbine engines shrieked to life.

The jet rolled forward, taxied off the runway and moved past the C-130s.

"Come, Death, come," Axeundarth chanted.

Bach-Zelewski and the other commandos looked on, silent, utterly still.

Wind soughed through the gorge.

Axeundarth knelt and drew target acquisition. Upmann smoke wreathed his face as he puffed on the cigar. A trickle of his previous victim's blood dripped off his chin.

The jet angled back onto the runway. It had another hundred yards to go before reaching the bend in the airstrip. There the jet could straighten out for takeoff through the mouth of the gorge.

It never made the bend.

When Axeundarth squeezed the RPG's trigger, the 85 mm projectile streaked away in a sizzling line of smoke and flame. The warhead impacted against the cockpit.

The German lowered the rocket launcher, watched as the fireball mushroomed into the sky. Then, quickly, he turned the remaining twin-turbine jets into fiery scrap with well-placed RPG warheads.

The gunships would remain undamaged. The C-130s belonged to him. They were his, and his alone.

Axeundarth faced Bach-Zelewski and the commandos, pitched the RPG-7 to the side. Walking toward the motionless group of men, he puffed leisurely on his cigar.

"I have no use for men who turn and run when things become difficult. Besides, the Arabs have the pilots of those gunships," Axeundarth said. "Let's see that we get them back. Alive."

Bach-Zelewski nodded, indicating that he understood.

But, of course, the East German understood, Axeundarth thought. Not to understand meant to die.

And Guntar Axeundarth was in a killing mood.

COLD VENGEANCE MOTIVATED Mack Bolan on his killing hunt. Jack Grimaldi's face stayed branded on his mind. His friend and ally through the years of hellfire was dead. But not forgotten. Not by a long shot.

One final, sweeping mop-up of the cannibals gathered here would help atone for the death of his friend. A little.

A lump caught in Bolan's throat. Death of a friend or loved one was always so goddamn bitter. Particularly, for some reason, when they had given their lives for the good fight. Not that Bolan had expected Grimaldi to live forever. It was just that there was so much that needed to be done, so many wrongs that needed to be righted. Grimaldi was a hell of a warrior. Bolan was going to miss him. Bad.

They were three hundred yards ahead, and Bolan was hell-bent on cutting the distance as quickly as possible. The gorge snaked past boulders and jagged slabs of rock, and he had followed the tortuous trail to the southeast—pursuing the survivors. Bolan was determined to make them regret that they had lived through the great battle in the gorge.

Bolan stuck to the higher ground, following his quarry on a parallel course. He was a little more than a hundred feet above them and a hundred fifty to two hundred yards behind them. The sun had climbed clear of the far-reaching fiery-white horizon, and Bolan kept the fireball to his back.

Silenced Beretta in hand, Bolan swiftly cut the gap between him and his prey by another fifty yards. The killing party ahead was well within range of the Beretta.

Crouched, Bolan angled down a gully. The enemy below had reached the end of the ravine and had stopped. They were a mixed bag of Arabs and Germans, and they had been squabbling about something for the past hour. Bolan couldn't make out the heated exchanges, but he guessed they were bickering about Fein Husra and where the pilots of the C-130s would have been taken.

Two Germans moved away from the mouth of the ravine, knelt and touched the rocky soil. Tire tracks. One of them pointed east. The other scanned the terrain through binoculars.

Bolan counted eighteen goons. This wasn't going to be easy, but it was sure as hell necessary. Bolan knew he'd be in trouble if he couldn't get their water, and he needed those binoculars.

The warrior folded down the small front handgrip on the Beretta, hooked his left thumb through the extended trigger guard for extra control and squeezed twice.

Two 9 mm slugs chugged from the silencer and drilled through the backs of two Arabs. They toppled without a sound. Before the others were alerted to the approach of sudden death, the Executioner triggered three lightning rounds.

Then, as three dead men reeled to the barren earth, voices shouted in alarm.

Bolan sent more terror into the savage horde. Lifting the M-16 to his shoulder, he triggered the M-203. The soldiers were scrambling for cover, but an unlucky foursome was rooted to the spot for a split second, searching the walls of the ravine for the invisible hitter.

A 40 mm hellbomb uprooted them—permanently. Survivors of the blast were spraying the walls of the ravine on both sides with wild autofire.

Bolan was already hustling for the higher ground. He came to a level stretch that led to a point directly above the rapidly diminishing enemy numbers.

"Who the fuck is out there?"

"Where the hell is the son of a bitch?"

"How should I know?"

"Shut up! Get your heads right. He has to be somewhere above us."

Right you are, Bolan thought, plucking two MK-2 frag grenades off his webbing.

"You three move out."

"Why should it be us, my German friend?"

Bolan pulled the pin and pitched the grenade into the cluster of men seventy feet below them.

The first shrapnel blast ended the bitching.

The second MK-2 dropped behind five soldiers, cutting off their hasty retreat. The explosion kicked three of them off their feet, razoring steel bits through their clothes and into their flesh.

Two wounded men cried out in pain.

Through the swirling dust, Bolan made out their figures. He switched the M-16 to single-shot mode, triggered two rounds. Their sounds of misery became death gurgles as 5.56 mm slugs punched between their shoulder blades.

Bolan drew a deep breath. Fein Husra and Dietl were next on his list of savages to be terminated.

Bolan checked the ravine behind him. Black cones of rock jutted up out of the range to the north.

The ridge leveled off into a plateau about a hundred yards to the north. Beyond that was a broken line of stone and boulder that stretched for a good half mile. It was treacherous turf, just the kind of place where an unseen enemy could observe him.

It took Bolan fifteen minutes to make his way down the gully, reach the mouth of the ravine. There, he stripped an Arab of a canteen and drank some of the tepid water quickly. His thirst quenched, the warrior then took the binoculars from one of the dead Germans.

"Striker! Striker!"

Bolan snapped his head sideways.

"Up here!"

He peered at the high ground to the west in disbelief. The man in the distance waved his arms.

Bolan looked through the high-powered Zeiss binoculars, then adjusted the focus.

"I'll be damned," Bolan breathed, unable to suppress a smile.

Grimaldi's battered face showed up clearly through the lenses.

"Don't just stand there like you've seen a ghost, big guy," Grimaldi called out. "What the hell, did you forget about parachutes?"

Bolan chuckled.

Then it happened. So suddenly that Grimaldi had no time to react.

The brief reunion was interrupted by sudden violence.

Bolan had no time to yell a warning.

The group of men converged on Grimaldi, seeming to boil up behind the ace pilot from out of nowhere.

"Jack!"

Autofire blazed down the ravine at the Executioner.

Chips of stone spitting at his face, Bolan ducked for cover behind the wall of the ravine's mouth. Crouching, he chanced a look around the corner, saw the rifle butts clubbing Grimaldi over the head. Grimaldi dropped at the feet of his attackers.

"Come, Bolan, come! I want you! You want your friend, you come and get him."

The taunting German voice echoed through the ravine. It was either Bach-Zelewski or his hired gun. Bolan couldn't be sure which.

More autofire chattered in the distance. Slugs hosed the floor of the ravine near Bolan, raising puffs of dust several feet from his face. Bullets whined off the rock above his head.

Damn! Out of the frying pan and into the hellfire. Again.

Bolan checked the ravine directly ahead: a narrow gully climbed up the slope of the canyon. He had to chance the run, and broke from cover.

If they got Grimaldi now, Bolan knew he might never see his friend alive again.

Autofire rained down behind him, but he was racing for the gully at breakneck speed and had caught the enemy during a lull in their suppressing fire.

Then the air *carumphed*, whistled with incoming mortars. The mouth of the gorge erupted behind Bolan in a series of flashing explosions.

Bolan reached cover in the gully.

Without hesitation, the Executioner scurried up the path, loading the M-203 on the run.

Grimaldi was on his mind.

And so was the extermination of more savages.

21

Grimaldi couldn't believe that someone had got the jump on him twice in such a short period of time. Some reunion with the big guy, he thought bitterly, then felt the warm trickle of blood running down the back of his neck. The sons of bitches had whacked him a few good ones, but he was still conscious. And as long as he was alive and kicking he'd go down fighting.

One of the goons had sliced the strap off his assault rifle and tied him up with it, and Grimaldi felt the leather binding bite deep into his wrists.

They hauled him to his feet.

"Move it! *Schnell! Schnell!*"

A kick in the butt sent Grimaldi stumbling ahead.

"You stay behind with three men," he heard the scar-faced killer order through the ringing in his ears. "Keep Bolan pinned down. If there's a way in here, there's a way out. You give us at least fifteen minutes."

"Are you saying to cover you while you escape?"

"What else would I be saying, dammit!"

Out of the corner of his eye, Grimaldi saw Bach-Zelewski sneer. Then he glanced at Axeundarth. He didn't think it was possible, but he actually believed the German assassin was either flustered or scared.

"I didn't know you were in charge here."

"Damn you, this is no time to argue. I will use this," Axeundarth said, shaking Grimaldi briefly as if he were nothing more than a wet rag, "to bring Bolan to me. I will kill him. I will kill them both."

"So you say."

"Just do as I tell you!"

Bach-Zelewski scanned the plateau.

"Take cover," he ordered three of the German commandos. Then: "I am out of rounds for the grenade launcher," he said to Axeundarth, whose face reddened with fury.

"I don't want you to kill him! Just keep him from advancing too quickly."

With that, Axeundarth shoved Grimaldi ahead.

"You bastard," the pilot spit through his bloodied mouth.

Axeundarth slapped Grimaldi across the back of his head with an open hand. "Shut up! Or I'll throw you into the ravine right now."

Grimaldi struggled to keep his balance. Bile rose into his throat, and he tasted the blood in his mouth. His head pounded relentlessly.

And he wondered just how much more punishment he could take.

A lot, he knew. However much he was asked to endure.

Because Striker was coming for him.

BOLAN SAW BACH-ZELEWSKI and his three goons take up positions behind the boulders at the far edge of the plateau. The enemy hadn't spotted Bolan.

The Executioner had followed the gully, seen the German assassin and his horde move off in the distance with Grimaldi.

The game was being played out to its deadly conclusion.

If he lost Grimaldi now...

Bolan checked the terrain. It was a good hundred yards across a stretch of wide open space to the enemy. They had been so busy surveying the floor of the ravine that Bach-Zelewski and his guns were still unaware that Bolan was now only a football field's distance away.

A wall of rock formed a half ring around the plateau to the west. There were enough jagged slabs of rock along the rimrock to give Bolan the necessary cover to come up on the enemy's right flank. The question was how to get up there.

Bolan found it.

Behind him, the gully sloped away gently. Crouched, he padded down the slope, came to a sharp wall of protruding rock that would act as a shield.

With his M-16 slung over his shoulder, Bolan crawled up the incline behind the rock wall. He found a series of nooks and cracks that served as steppingstones, and he climbed the wall. Once there he lay outstretched on his stomach. He had a clear view of the enemy. Their heads showed, inches above the cover of their boulders. Bolan realized it would be difficult, if not impossible, to take them all out from this distance and at his present angle.

Silently he crabbed along the ridge, losing sight of the hired killer and his hunting party. Bolan assumed Bach-Zelewski and his guns had been ordered to stay behind to buy time for the contract killer.

What they bought for themselves was a one-way ticket to hell.

Bolan closed the gap between himself and his targets to fifty feet. Big Thunder filled his fist. He drew target acquisition on the goon closest to him and fired.

The AutoMag roared and bucked in Bolan's fist. He rode out the recoil, saw the .44 slug plow through the right ear of his first target. As blood and brains washed over the next goon in line, Bolan squeezed off another round, the .44 slug coring through another skull, turning bone and brain into erupting mush. A face of shock and fear swung into Bolan's deathsights next, and the Executioner obliterated that frozen look with a pulverizing .44 headbuster.

Bach-Zelewski raked Bolan's position with a quick Uzi burst. As lead whined off the rimrock, the warrior threw himself into a roll. He stopped behind a boulder, then got to his feet, firing the AutoMag two-handed.

Two thundering 240-grain boattails drilled through Bach-Zelewski's chest. The double .44 impact punched Bach-Zelewski toward the edge of the plateau. The Uzi subgun flew away from his hands, clattered down the side of the canyon wall. He remained spread-eagled, his head, arms and torso dangling over the lip of the plateau. The East German's arms twitched in death throes.

Swiftly Bolan moved down the ridge. He didn't care if the hired killer heard the peals of the killing shots. In fact, Bolan wanted the man to hear them.

He wanted the assassin to know he was coming for him.

For thirty minutes, Bolan stuck to the high ground until he found another gully that led him down into the ravine. Fifteen minutes earlier he had spotted the assassin's killing party. They came to a narrow passage that led them out of the canyon.

Bolan figured they had a good thirty-minute jump on him. Every step for him, though, became marked by caution. Uncertain if gunmen were laying in wait, he kept close to the wall of the ravine, using boulders when he came to them and stopping to check the high ground for a glint of sunlight off a weapon that would betray the position of a hidden marksman.

There was nothing else in the canyon—other than the dead.

Bolan's wary trek cost him valuable time.

When he finally reached the passage, he discovered that his quarry was almost lost to sight, running across the far-reaching, flat emptiness of the desert.

They were headed due east.

Bolan moved out of the canyon and angled off to the north, determined to either head off the killing party, or come up on them from their left flank.

Just one more mile.

One more mile in hell.

Bolan checked the sky. The sun was already a giant orange fireball. Sweat soaked Bolan's blacksuit, and large beads of moisture rolled down his face. He squinted, the salty wetness burning into his eyes.

He set out, loping away from the mountains. Behind the Executioner, vultures filled the sky.

Scavengers.

There was plenty of carrion back there to feed them. For a long time to come.

And Mack Bolan intended to give the vultures more dead meat to devour.

DIETL DECIDED it was time to take charge. Waiting in the *gassi*, the wind-formed lane between the sand dunes, was fraying the German armorer's nerves. He had exactly twenty-one gunmen left—as opposed to Fein Husra's ragtag crew of forty-five.

At the moment, nobody was doing a thing—except waiting and sweating in the brutal heat of the Sahara. From its noonday zenith, the sun blazed off the white sand; the *gassi* was a furnace. Dietl was about to explode with rage. Worse, he couldn't get rid of the black flies that swarmed around his face. Annoyed, feeling his fury and impatience mounting by the moment, Dietl swatted at the flies, cursing viciously.

''This is bullshit,'' Dietl growled at Fein Husra.

Husra was lounging against the front of the APC. Dietl found it hard to believe that most of the Arabs were now spending their time trying to shade themselves from the fireball in the sky. The pilots were in the bed of the APC, and Dietl couldn't see the sense in twenty to thirty heavily armed men hanging around the APC guarding six unarmed fly-boys. Particularly when the Arabs were crowding Dietl's own space and threatening to shove him out into the fiery sunshine. He wrinkled his nose and thought he would gag. They smelled bad. Dietl had never been able to tolerate anybody's body odor but his own.

"What is bullshit?" Fein Husra returned, nerves taut.

"The way your people just lounge around like they were on vacation," Dietl said, arms folded over his chest, back braced against the side of the APC, "while my men make sure sentry duty is fulfilled. It is a good thing somebody here has some sense."

Husra chuckled. "Dietl, don't worry. There is nobody out there. Miles and miles of nothing. We would see them coming from a good two miles out."

"How the hell would you know anybody's coming? You're down here."

"Have you forgotten the war back in the gorge? Surely they should have wiped each other out by now. All we must do is go back there and smell the scent of death and destruction. Yes...a small glimpse at what our future missions in Europe shall look like."

"Well, this waiting is killing me. I have the best guns for a thousand miles in any direction," Dietl said, uncapping his canteen, gulping large swallows of warm water. "Let me tell you this. As soon as darkness comes tonight, we move out. With or without you. And I'm taking those pilots."

Anger flickered through Husra's dark stare, then he smiled. "Certainly. We shall go in tonight and leave in the C-130s."

"I think I have something over here."

Dietl and Husra looked up the slopes. Along the crest of the dunes, Dietl's men were stretched out in prone positions. With Zeiss binoculars, they scanned the barren wasteland.

Dietl and Husra trudged up the slope. At the top, Dietl crouched beside Weir, a former GSG-9 man.

"What is it?"

Weir handed Dietl the binocs. The German armorer wiped sweat off his brow with the back of his hand. The heat was unbearable, and Dietl felt himself becoming more irritated by the second.

"There."

Dietl looked through the lenses, to the west. A little more than a mile in that direction, the sandy desert floor ended, leveled off into gravel plain. The sand dunes to the west gradually leveled out, and Dietl could just barely make out the smoke curling from the wreckage of the twin-turbine jets they had stumbled across last night. Whoever had landed in those jets had been responsible for launching the surprise attack. In a way, Dietl knew it was a damn good thing the mystery enemy had struck when they did. Otherwise, Dietl and his men might have been slaughtered by the attackers who had hidden in the C-130.

The Arabs down in the *gassi* were stirred from their lethargy, and they stood looking up the slope at Dietl and Husra.

"What is it?" one of the Arabs called up to his leader.

"Nothing," the Palestinian answered, "I don't see anything there."

"I would have sworn I saw movement," Weir muttered.

"My German friend," Fein Husra said, "the sun and the heat can sometimes play tricks on your eyes."

"It was no mirage, dammit!" Weir snarled.

Dietl lowered the binocs. He checked the dunes to the east, north and south. They had ridden in from the east, and the tire tracks of the APC were obvious in the sand and even in the hard-packed soil of the gravel plain, if an experienced tracker looked closely enough. It would not take much effort or experience, though, for an assault party to snake its way over the burning dunes and creep up on the *gassi*.

Suddenly Dietl was worried. The choice of this stronghold had seemed logical at the time. But now he felt otherwise. They could easily be encircled, trapped and picked off like rats in a barrel.

"Weir, I want you to take some of your men. If you think you saw something, I believe you did. Go out there and check."

Weir nodded. He turned, whistled across the *gassi* for his men.

Moments later, the recon party set out.

Dietl watched them move out. He drew a deep breath, sighing loudly.

Fein Husra appeared amused as he looked at Dietl. "You seem nervous, my friend."

"I'm not your friend. Let's get that straight. This is business and only business."

The terrorist grinned. "Merely a figure of speech."

"Save it."

Binocs pressed to his eyes, Dietl scanned the dunes.

Weir's men spread out. One man dropped behind the group, surveying the distant crests of the dunes to the south through field glasses. Two men guarded the flanks.

"I don't like it," Dietl muttered. "Something doesn't feel right. Something..."

Dietl's mouth dropped. The binocs fell away from his eyes.

They had come in from the south.

"Weir!"

But it was too late to warn the recon party.

Autofire rained down on Weir and his men. A grenade sailed away from the dune that covered the attackers, dropped dead center in the line of Weir's commandos. The explosion ripped through the heart of the men, scattering bits and pieces of flesh and cloth over the brilliant white sheen of sand.

Then Dietl heard the familiar and suddenly very terrifying whistle of incoming mortars.

"You call this nothing?" Dietl rasped, Husra scrambling to his feet, wheeling and running down the slope.

Explosions pounded into the *gassi*.

The air screamed with deafening blasts that raked the sand dunes.

Dietl stumbled, rolled down the slope.

Arabs scattered, racing pell-mell up the dune, but there was nowhere to run.

Dietl hit the bottom of the slope. He looked up and saw attackers in black common fatigues pop over the crest of the dune to the east.

The Arabs trying to flee the *gassi* ran head-on into the enemy.

Into a wall of roaring autofire.

22

The stalk and destroy had worked exactly as Guntar Axeundarth had planned. They had picked up the tire tracks of the APC, and had followed them to what was left of Axeundarth's squad of jets.

The fly-boy had turned those jets to smoking junk. Axeundarth had knocked Grimaldi down and kicked him a few times in the face and ribs for such "senseless destruction." He might have killed Grimaldi on the spot, but he knew the pilot would prove useful later—Axeundarth planned to have Grimaldi fly him out of the Sahara in one of the C-130s. There was at least enough fuel to get them all to Algiers. Once there, the assassin could hire pilots to come back and fly the other two C-130s to him at a designated rendezvous site.

But now, Axeundarth had his mind set on slaughter.

Atop the crest of the dune to the south of the APC, Axeundarth shoved Grimaldi to the ground, spearing his knee into the pilot's back, pinning him to the sand.

Axeundarth cut loose with his Uzi submachine gun. The mortar barrage had created a hell of confusion and death down in the *gassi*. To the north, seven of

Axeundarth's commandos were hosing the Arabs with long bursts of autofire. Screaming, the terrorists spun, blood spurting from their chests. They tumbled down the slope, blood trailing their flopping corpses.

The assassin sprayed the Arabs near the APC with long sweeping bursts of 9 mm parabellum slugs. Three more 40 mm hellbombs sizzled through the air behind Axeundarth's six commandos, all of whom were drilling Weir and his recon party into the sand with merciless autofire. The trio of explosions boiled through a troop of Arabs running to jump into the bed of the APC. It was a stupid move on their part. Even if they had reached the APC they would eventually have been trapped there.

The mortar bombardment ended.

Axeundarth's commandos surged past the butchered recon party. The German rammed a fresh 32-round clip into his Uzi as Grimaldi struggled to break free beneath him. Axeundarth dug his knee into the pilot's back.

"Stay still," the assassin yelled over the din of weapons fire, the Uzi blazing in his fists, "or I'll blow your brains out!"

Moments later, both killteams were in position on opposite sides of the *gassi*. Scissoring autofire pulped the remaining Arabs to bloody meat. Caught out in the open and sandwiched between twin lines of autofire, the Arabs didn't stand a chance against such a furious fusillade of lead. Their bodies slammed off the hull of the APC, slugs whining off the lead-plated sides.

Axeundarth stopped firing. "Move in!" he ordered the team beside him, waving his arm.

Half the commandos began moving down the slope as wounded Arabs, lying on the ground, moaning in pain, were chewed up by a final blistering leadstorm.

The shots echoed across the dunes behind Axeundarth. Bodies twitched around the APC.

He stood and pulled Grimaldi off the sand.

Then the German assassin heard the roar of automatic weapons fire. He watched along the crest of the north dune as his commandos were shredded by bullets that zipped up their legs, backs and heads. Blood and brains washed over the white sand as skulls erupted. Several hideously wounded commandos screamed in pain.

Bolan, Axeundarth knew. He had not forgotten about the Executioner, but he hadn't expected him to make such a sudden, swift and deadly appearance. Bach-Zelewski and the others had failed. And obviously they had paid for their failure.

The commandos beside Axeundarth were halfway down the slope. They froze for a split second at the sight of their brothers-in-arms being slaughtered. Then they turned, started to charge back up the slope for cover.

It was the wrong move to make.

Mack Bolan hit a combat crouch behind the commandos he'd killed. A mini-Uzi in each hand, he opened up on the retreating soldiers. With deadly pinpoint mini-Uzi fire, Bolan cut the men down as they ran up the slope.

Then, at the edge of his field of fire, Bolan saw Grimaldi barrel into the scar-faced assassin as the hired killer attempted to draw target acquisition.

Axeundarth stumbled away from Grimaldi, who pitched facefirst into the sand.

As Axeundarth shuffled sideways, he triggered a short burst at Bolan.

Sand spit up at Bolan's face. But the return fire was coming from another direction, and he swept a short burst with both Uzis at Axeundarth. Short, but accurate.

Flinching as lead tore across his shoulder, Bolan dropped behind the crest.

A cry of pain ripped from Axeundarth's lips. He spun, toppled to the sand.

Grimaldi clambered to his feet. "Mack!" he yelled. "The front of the truck!"

Axeundarth rolled sideways down the dune, a line of crimson streaking the white sand behind him.

Weapons fire blazed over the hood of the APC.

Bolan hustled down behind the crest of the dune, plucking an MK-2 off his webbing as he ran.

Moments later, when the Executioner was directly behind the APC, he saw two of the pilots scrambling out of its bed. They were sure they were safe behind the APC now that all visible combatants were dead.

Except for Bolan.

The Executioner pulled the pin on the frag grenade and hurled it down into the *gassi*. It hit the sand beneath the APC's tailgate and rolled under the frame of the armored personnel carrier.

A second later, Bolan charged down the slope, AutoMag snaking away from quick-draw leather on his right hip. A heartbeat, and the frag grenade blew, spitting out smoke, flames, sand and lethal metal fragments that scythed through the legs of the pilots hiding behind the vehicle.

Bodies were propelled away from the APC by the deafening blast, howls of agony lancing the air.

The Executioner stepped into the hellzone.

Four of the six pilots lay on the ground, nothing more than torn and twisted bloody sacks. Two had survived the explosion. They were covered in blood.

With glassy eyes, one of the pilots stared up at Bolan as the Executioner stood over him. "P-please...listen...help us...we can fly you out of here..."

Bolan lifted the AutoMag. "No, thanks. I already have a pilot."

Bolan squeezed Big Thunder's trigger. The thunder of the killing shots pealed across the dunes.

Bolan scanned the killzone. Nothing moved. There was utter silence.

As he sheathed Big Thunder, Grimaldi walked down the slope. Bolan looked at his friend's brutally battered face. Grimaldi had been through hell, but the guy was a fighter. There was no quit in him.

He had never been happier to see Grimaldi.

Bolan fisted his commando dagger and smiled at his friend.

"You look like hell, Jack."

"Thanks, Striker," Grimaldi growled. He grinned, and winced. "You don't look so hot, either."

Bolan glanced at his shoulder. Blood was seeping into his blacksuit, but the bullet had only nicked his shoulder. "I've felt better."

"I hear ya. Hell, I don't know about you, but I'm ready to go home. I could use about three days' shut-eye."

"You got it. I'll even buy the beer," Bolan remarked dryly.

Now Grimaldi smiled without grimacing. "You're a heck of a guy."

"WHAT'S THE MATTER, MACK?"

They were a half klick west of the jet wreckage that lay on the desert floor. The flaming sun seemed to spread a glowing white sheet over the gravel plain and the sand dunes to the east. The air was parched, and it was difficult to breathe.

"I can't shake the feeling we're being followed."

Concern hardened Grimaldi's eyes. He toted Bolan's M-16.

"How could that be? The only thing we left behind us was a few dozen dead men."

Bolan sucked in a deep breath. He was stiff, sore, exhausted. But as bad as he felt, he knew his friend was in far worse shape. Bolan had already checked Jack's injuries and found four cracked ribs. Grimaldi would also need a good number of stitches to close the wounds to the back of his head. But the guy hadn't uttered a word of complaint. Bitching just wasn't Grimaldi's style.

Bolan checked the desert through his Zeiss binoculars.

Grimaldi sucked water from one of Bolan's captured canteens.

Bolan found nothing in any direction but a shimmering heat mist. Still, he had that itch, right between his shoulder blades. The same damn feeling he got when he suspected he was lined up in an enemy marksman's cross hairs.

It stood to reason, Bolan knew, that out of all the men who had fought here in the Sahara, someone had survived the fierce battles. Or played possum.

"Let's just get back to that gorge, Striker, and get the hell outta here."

Bolan nodded. Sound advice. There was really nothing left here in the Algerian Sahara for them to do, except to either destroy the C-130s they couldn't fly out or make arrangements in Algiers for Uncle Sam to have the gunships brought back.

Bolan opted for the latter.

"Yeah," Bolan agreed. "Let's go."

They walked on.

Plumes of black smoke rose into the sky behind them.

Bolan wasn't convinced that there was no enemy out there.

The itch between the Executioner's shoulder blades spread.

HE PUT ONE FOOT in front of the other. He felt wooden, immobile. Every step came with a concentrated act of will.

There was no other way.

He was in terrible pain. Pain unlike anything he had ever experienced.

He was drenched in sweat and his own blood. A fever raged in his brain.

Kill Bolan. Kill Bolan.

He thought his lips were moving as he heard the voice in his head urge him on to vengeance.

To avoid total disaster. To ward off the looming prospect of such humiliating defeat.

He dropped to his knees, overcome by pain. He felt his lips part, and he wanted to vomit.

But there was nothing in his stomach to throw up.

How could this have happened to him? he wondered. Rage and bitter hatred tore through his guts. He felt his insides twist with the acrid sting of bile, a burning but hollow sensation that reached from his stomach to his throat.

He must go the final few miles.

He must.

To stop now meant to lose. And to lose meant to die.

He climbed to his feet. The sun burning down on the back of his neck, he plodded onward.

One foot in front of the other.

Kill Bolan. Must... kill Bolan.

EPILOGUE

The gorge was silent.

Bolan and Grimaldi stepped into the abyss of death.

Walls of black smoke drifted across the compound on a low, moaning wind. Bolan and Grimaldi stood in the mouth of the gorge for a long moment. It was hard to believe the carnage.

"It will never end, Mack, you know that? Scenes like this sometimes make me wonder just where the hell it's all headed."

Bolan nodded. Yeah, he understood what Jack was saying, all right. When men lived at the expense of the lives of others, this was how they ended up. This was how they *deserved* to end up. How many times had Bolan seen it? How many more times would he see it?

Eyes peeled for any sign of movement, Bolan and Grimaldi slowly walked toward the C-130s.

Grimaldi stepped over a discarded RPG-7, expelling a deep breath. He teetered for a second on rubbery legs.

Bolan looked at his friend, concerned. "You going to be all right, Jack?"

"Yeah, yeah. Just a little headache." He rested a hand wearily on Bolan's shoulder. "Don't worry, I'll get us home."

Minutes later, they closed on the lead C-130. Both men stood by the fuselage door.

"Where to?"

"Algiers. We'll get in touch with Brognola. He'll send some people here to pick up the Hercs."

"And pick up the pieces."

Bolan nodded. He reached to open the fuselage door, but heard a scraping noise from somewhere behind. Snapping his head sideways, Bolan spotted the crouching figure instantly.

Axeundarth raised the RPG-7 to his shoulder.

Bolan and Grimaldi raced from the C-130 just as Axeundarth triggered the warhead. A heartbeat later, the 85 mm projectile slammed into the fuselage door.

They nose-dived to the ground.

The airplane was cut in two as the fireball boiled through the fuselage.

Wreckage blew over Bolan's head as he leaped to his feet, Big Thunder streaking from his holster.

Grimaldi came up firing with his M-16.

Bolan pumped two thundering rounds into Axeundarth's chest. As the .44 rounds pounded the German to his back, a line of 5.56 mm tumblers were stitching up his stomach, chest and face.

Grimaldi emptied the whole magazine into Axeundarth's writhing body.

Bolan and Grimaldi stood, side by side, grim-faced. The twisted hull of the C-130 blazed behind them.

"I owed that bastard," Grimaldi rasped through clenched teeth.

"I'd say you paid him back. In spades."

Grimaldi flung the M-16 away.